CODE OF PORTRAYAL

Robert Fucilla

Published 2011 by arima publishing
www.arimapublishing.com

ISBN 978 1 84549 503 9
© Robert Fucilla 2011

Printed and bound in the United Kingdom
Typeset in Palatino Linotype, 11pt

Swirl is an imprint of arima publishing.
arima publishing
ASK House, Northgate Avenue
Bury St Edmunds, Suffolk IP32 6BB
t: (+44) 01284 700321
www.arimapublishing.com

FADE IN:

1 - SUPERIMPOSE:

CALABRIA – ITALY

1929

IN BLACK AND WHITE.

2 - INT. CORRIDOR. NIGHT.

A HUGE MAN, in uniform, walks down a dimly lit corridor. He holds a ROPE, one end of which is knotted to form a noose. He stops outside a door and produces a bunch of keys. He unlocks the door and enters.

From within we hear sounds of a struggle then a CRACK and

SILENCE.

The door opens and the HUGE MAN emerges. As he comes out we Catch a glimpse of a another MAN hanging from the ceiling. The rope is around his neck. The MAN is still.

FADE TO.

3 - START CREDITS.

4 - EXT. CALABRIA. MORNING.

LONG SHOT.   The Village of COSENZA set in the valleys.   A HORSEMAN rides at a fast pace towards the village.

BACK TO COLOUR.

CLOSE UP. The HORSEMAN – this is FRANCESCO ACCIARDI, rides. In the background we see the beautiful mountains dell' Aspromonte.

5 - SUPERIMPOSE:

CALABRIA - ITALY

1939

CUT TO:

6 - EXT. COSENZA. MORNING.

FOUR OLD PEOPLE sitting at a table playing cards, outside a bar. They look up as FRANCESCO gallops past them.

As FRANCESCO rides through the streets we see POSTERS of BENITO MUSSOLINI on the walls.

CUT TO:

7 - EXT. BARBER SHOP. MORNING.

As FRANCESCO rides up to the barbershop he sees a queue waiting outside. Next to the barbershop there is a Tailor's shop. Outside the Tailor's there are two APRENTICES working on black shirts. The TAILOR also works on a black shirt.

The TAILOR lifts a needle up to his eye. His POV: Through the eye of the needle he sees FRANCESCO tie up his horse to a wall ring.

TAILOR

Francesco, business is good, eh?

FRANCESCO

Ruggiero's getting married tomorrow. They want to look their best, no?

FRANCESCO opens the door and the queue file into the shop.

CUT TO:

8 - EXT. DE'ANDRIA MANSION. EVENING.

THE MANSION has huge grounds girdled by a rich dirt bridle path, stables and pasture for a herd of horses. The hedges, flowerbeds, and grasses are cut to perfection.

CUT TO:

9 - INT. DE'ANDRIA MANSION. DINING ROOM. EVENING.

The table is set for dinner. DON LUCIANO DE'ANDRIA – in his fifties, is at the head of the table. At the opposite end sits his wife, MAFALDA. On one side of the table sits his daughter, MARIA. She sits next to a MAN in uniform. He wears a BLACK SHIRT – this is RICARDO PACULA (Pacula should be of the same age as Don De'Andria). On the other side of the table sits a priest – this is PADRE PINO.

SERVANTS move in and out of the table as they serve dinner.

DON DE'ANDRIA

Padre Pino, I am so pleased you could make it this evening.

PADRE PINO

It is my pleasure. But you shouldn't have gone to all this trouble just for me.

PACULA

(cuts in)

Nonsense, Padre. Nothing is too good for the priest who is going to bless our marriage.

PACULA turns to MARIA.

Don't you agree, Maria?

PADRE PINO looks at MARIA, expecting her to answer.

MARIA

(anxiously)

Of course.

PADRE PINO notices MARIA'S anxiety.

PADRE PINO

Is there something the matter my child?

MARIA

No, Padre Pino. Please excuse me for a moment.

MARIA stands. They all look at her.

MARIA leaves the room. DON DE'ANDRIA nods to MAFALDA. MAFALDA stands. PADRE PINO curiously watches her leave the room.

DON DE'ANDRIA attracts PADRE PINO'S attention.

DON DE'ANDRIA

So, Padre Pino shall we discuss the wedding arrangements?

SILENCE. Then,

PADRE PINO

Yes, of course.

CUT TO:

<u>10 - INT. MARIA'S BEDROOM. EVENING.</u>

MARIA is on a bed. She sobs quietly into a pillow. MAFALDA DE'ANDRIA, comforts her. Another WOMAN – this is ANNA; Maria's governess, stands at the foot of the bed.

MAFALDA

Maria, you must come down. Your father will be very angry. You know the way he is.

MARIA

I don't care, mama. I will never marry, Ricardo Pacula. I would sooner die than marry him.

MAFALDA turns and looks at ANNA.

CUT TO:

11 - INT. DE'ANDRIA MANSION. DINING ROOM. EVENING.
The three MEN are in deep conversation as the door opens and ANNA enters. She walks over to DON DE'ANDRIA.

ANNA

Maria regrets that she will not be able to return. She is not feeling well.

DON DE'ANDRIA

Is my wife with her?

ANNA

Yes.

DON DE'ANDRIA waves her away. ANNA exits. DON DE'ANDRIA and PACULA exchange a look.

PACULA

What is going on? I thought everything had been settled.

DON DE'ANDRIA

And it is my dear friend. It is. Excuse me for a moment.

DON DE'ANDRIA leaves the table and exits. PACULA remains silent, staring impassively at PADRE PINO. As the silence continues, PACULA feels obliged to make further conversation.

PACULA

She's just a little nervous, Padre.

PADRE PINO

Naturally.

(beat)

Tell me General Pacula, do you think our alliance with Germany will be good for Italy?

PACULA

Yes. Italy will prosper. We will be strong again.

PADRE PINO

But surely we are heading for war now Hitler has invaded Poland.

PACULA

Sometimes a war is needed for so many different reasons. After all The Roman Empire once ruled the world. They didn't achieve that without a few invasions here and there.

PACULA LAUGHS. But PADRE PINO remains SILENT.

CUT TO:

12 - INT. FRANCESCO'S HOME. EVENING.

The room is shabby. It has the look of a man living on his own, and in desperation of a woman's touch. FRANCESCO is asleep on a bed. He moans in his sleep.

FRANCESCO

No. Don't papa. Don't!

SIX GUNSHOTS are heard, simultaneously.

As he awakes he springs to an upright position, still

SCREAMING:

Don't!

CLOSE ON HIS FACE. His eyes wide, staring. Perspiration trickles down the side of his face from his forehead.

CUT TO:

13 - EXT. MARIA'S BEDROOM. EVENING.

Door opens. DON DE'ANDRIA enters. MAFALDA turns to the door.

MAFALDA

She's just a little tired. She needs to rest.

DON DE'ANDRIA

We are downstairs discussing her future. She should be there.

MARIA immediately sits up and wipes her tearstained face.

MARIA

I have no future, papa. Not with Ricardo.

DON DE'ANDRIA

What is the matter with you, Maria? Haven't we already discussed this matter? And you agreed.

MAFALDA

No, Luciano, you agreed.

(beat)

Can't you see her heart is breaking?

DON DE'ANDRIA

You don't understand, Mafalda. So stay out of this.

Turns to MARIA.

Maria, compose yourself and come downstairs, please.

Without a word, MARIA follows her father out of the room. MAFALDA watches them leave.

CUT TO:

14 - EXT. TAILOR SHOP. MORNING.

The sky is cloudy. Through the shop window we see the TAILOR looking out up at the sky. Behind him FRANCESCO is trying on a new suit.

CUT TO:

15 - INT. TAILOR SHOP. MORNING.

The TAILOR looks out of the window.

TAILOR

(mutters)

Not a nice day for a wedding.

The TAILOR turns away from the window and faces FRANCESCO, who is admiring himself in a long mirror.

FRANCESCO

You did a fine job on this suit. Fits like a glove.

TAILOR

So when do I start on the finest suit Cosenza has ever seen?

FRANCESCO gives him a searching look.

For when you get married. You don't want to be the best man forever, do you? So when will it be?

FRANCESCO smiles.

FRANCESCO

Not for a long time. First I have to find someone who'll have me.

They both LAUGH. FRANCESCO exits.

CUT TO:

16 - EXT. TAILOR SHOP. MORNING.

FRANCESCO comes out. He crosses to his horse and unties it. He mounts and rides away.

CUT TO:

17 - EXT. CLIFF. AFTERNOON.

MARIA is on a WHITE HORSE. She slowly rides up to the cliffs' edge. She looks down. There is a stillness, as if life itself has been suspended. Neither bird nor animal make a sound.

ANNA is making her way slowly up the winding trail that leads to the cliff, letting the horse choose the pace.

From a distance FRANCESCO is watering his horse. He looks towards the cliffs' edge. His POV: MARIA turns away and rides slowly away from the edge and stops by a huge tree. She turns and faces the cliff edge. She bursts out crying.

FRANCESCO watches in amusement. Then his attention is drawn to a LIGHTNING FLICKER above the mountains.

MARIA feels a heavy drop of rain on her arm. She looks up and another drop hits her forehead and trickles down her face mingling with her own tears.

The stillness is suddenly split by an instant CRACK of THUNDER, then LIGHTNING.

The LIGHTNING strikes the huge tree. The flash causes the horse to rear up and bolt towards the cliffs' edge.
LONG SHOT. It is RAINING hard. MARIA'S horse is out of control, and heading for the cliffs' edge. She desperately holds on.

ANOTHER HORSE comes into SHOT - FRANCESCO is on this horse. It gains upon the unsettled WHITE HORSE. He moves along side the frightened WHITE HORSE and grabs the reins and expertly reins him in, getting control. He pulls him to a halt. He calms the WHITE HORSE.

FRANCESCO jumps down and as he lifts MARIA off the horse, another crack of THUNDER. The WHITE HORSE rears up again nudging FRANCESCO. He loses his balance and with MARIA he falls to the ground.

MARIA rolls over the cliff. FRANCESCO reacts fast, grabbing her hand as she goes over.

ANNA reaches the cliffs edge. She dismounts.

FRANCESCO is holding MARIA'S hand for all he is worth.
                    FRANCESCO
              Hold on! I've got you.

ANNA joins FRANCESCO and helps him pull MARIA to safety.

The rain comes down harder. ANNA and MARIA run to the safety of the tree. FRANCESCO calms the WHITE HORSE. He leads both horses to the tree. The side of the tree still SMOKES from the lightning bolt.
                      ANNA
          What were you doing up here?

MARIA ignores her. She watches FRANCESCO take off his jacket and wring it out. She approaches him.
                     MARIA
              Are you alright?

                    FRANCESCO
        Yeah, I'll make it but my suit won't.

FRANCESCO turns to her and sees her properly for the first time. Her beauty captivates him. He smiles.
                    FRANCESCO
          How about you? You okay?

MARIA

Yes. Thanks to you.

FRANCESCO

I'm Francesco Acciardi.

MARIA

Maria De'Andria. And this is Anna, my governess.

FRANCESCO smiles and nods at them both.
You must come back with us. Anna
will clean your suit.

FRANCESCO

Thanks. But I'm already late.

MARIA

Where are you going?

FRANCESCO

To a wedding.

MARIA'S eyes go down.

MARIA

Oh! I'm so sorry. I hope I haven't spoilt your wedding day.

FRANCESCO LAUGHS.

FRANCESCO

No. Not my wedding day. It's a friend of mine's. In Cosenza.

MARIA looks up again. She smiles.

MARIA

Then I insist you come back with us. You can't go to your friend's wedding looking like that.

MARIA turns to ANNA.

Anna we must do something about his suit.

ANNA turns to FRANCESCO but speaks to MARIA.

ANNA

Of course, Maria. That's the least we can do.

CUT TO:

18 - EXT. FIELD. AFTERNOON.

The rain has stopped and the sun is shining. ANNA rides in front. FRANCESCO and MARIA ride side by side, with no other sound but the rhythmic creak of their saddles. Neither of them seem to feel the need to talk. But now and then they look at each other.

CUT TO:

19 - EXT. DE'ANDRIA MANSION. GATES. AFTERNOON.

As ANNA rides through the gates and up toward the house, she looks back. Her POV: FRANCESCO and MARIA ride side by side. She notices a change in MARIA. It is almost as if MARIA has, at last, found a new meaning in life. ANNA can't help but slowly shake her head.

CUT TO:

20 - EXT. DE'ANDRIA MANSION. AFTERNOON.

As ANNA, MARIA, and FRANCESCO dismount, a SERVANT takes the horses and leads them to a stable.

From a window DON DE'ANDRIA looks out.

RICARDO PACULA comes out and goes to MARIA. He takes her hand. Reluctantly she lets him hold her hand.

PACULA

Where have you been? We were all worried about you.

His attention shifts to FRANCESCO.

MARIA

I went out for a ride with Anna.

FRANCESCO extends a hand to PACULA.

FRANCESCO

You must be Maria's father? Francesco Acciardi. Pleased to meet you.

PACULA ignores FRANCESCO'S hand and looks to ANNA.

ANNA

Maria had a little accident. Mr Acciardi came to her rescue.

PACULA

How terrible for you Maria. Let's go in and you can tell me all about it.

As PACULA leads her into the house, MARIA turns back.

MARIA

Anna please see to Francesco's suit.

MARIA then looks at FRANCESCO and smiles. FRANCESCO returns her smile.

CUT TO:

21 - INT. DE'ANDRIA MANSION. KITCHEN. AFTERNOON.

FRANCESCO sits sipping a hot drink. ANNA is pressing the suit.

FRANCESCO

I thought he was her father. He's old enough.

(to himself) She really was going to do it.

ANNA

That's not the first time.

FRANCESCO

She's tried before?

ANNA

Look I can't discuss this any further. Here's your suit. And if I were you I'd forget all about her. It can only lead to trouble.

FRANCESCO takes the suit and puts it on.

FRANCESCO

Trouble? For a woman like Maria a man would take on the world.

ANNA

You might have to.

FRANCESCO opens the door and exits.

CUT TO:

22 - INT. DE'ANDRIA MANSION. HALL. AFTERNOON.

As FRANCESCO walks down the hall MARIA meets him.

FRANCESCO

Look. Anna did a fine job. It's as good as new.

MARIA

I want to apologize for Ricardo's behavior.

FRANCESCO

No need. I understand. Look why don't you come to the wedding tonight. It's at Mazza's restaurant opposite the church in Cosenza.

MARIA

No. I couldn't possibly come. My father wouldn't allow it.

FRANCESCO

Then don't tell him.

(beat)

Try, please.

He smiles warmly at her. She looks into his eyes as if they were about to kiss when suddenly they hear FOOTSTEPS from around a corridor.

MARIA hurries off and disappears into a room leaving the door slightly open.

FRANCESCO walks towards the sound of the footsteps. As he rounds a corner he meets DON DE'ANDRIA and PACULA.

PACULA

This is the man who saved Maria.

FRANCESCO again extends a hand.

FRANCESCO

I hope I got it right this time.

FRANCESCO looks to PACULA then to DON DE'ANDRIA.
You must be Maria's father? Francesco Acciardi. Pleased to meet you.

Again his hand is ignored. PACULA notices the door which is slightly open, opens a little more.

PACULA

**Tell me Mr Acciardi what work
do you do?**

FRANCESCO

I'm a barber.

PACULA

A barber, eh? Does that pay you well?

FRANCESCO

I get by.

PACULA

A barber, eh?

FRANCESCO

It suits me for now.

PACULA

Well I suppose it's an honest trade and someone has to do it.

FRANCESCO

So?

PACULA

You said "for now". You seem an ambitious type though, perhaps you have greater plans for the future?

FRANCESCO looks at him with contempt. PACULA points at several paintings and busts of legendary Italian heroes in the hall.

PACULA

Look at the wealth that surrounds you, my dear barber. Do you ever think you could give all this to a woman?

DON DE'ANDRIA

(cuts in)

How long have you known my daughter?

FRANCESCO

Today. I met her for the first time today.

PACULA

Really?

FRANCESCO

Jesus! You sure know how to thank someone.

FRANCESCO turns and walks away. PACULA reacts.

PACULA

Why that impertinent peasant. How dare he turn his back on you!

DON DE'ANDRIA pulls PACULA back.

DON DE'ANDRIA

Let him go.

PACULA sees the door that Maria had left slightly open now quietly close. He smiles to himself.

CUT TO:

23 - EXT. COSENZA. AFTERNOON.

It is a beautiful day in the small town. Small cobbled stoned streets give way to closely built light grey houses on either side. In the distance we see FRANCESCO dressed in a black suit, riding his horse through the street.

FRANCESCO arrives at an open courtyard outside a small church. He dismounts from his horse and ties the reins to a tree, brushes the dust off his suit and runs up the stone steps to the church doors and enters.

CUT TO:

24 - INT. CHURCH. DAY.

FRANCESCO enters. He dips his fingers in a bowl then crosses himself.

The church is full. At the back, in a dark corner sits a WOMAN – this is LENA, she is dressed in black with a dark veil around her head.

As FRANCESCO goes by her they exchange a nod and a smile. LENA bows her head and continues to pray.

As FRANCESCO makes his way to the front, PEOPLE smile and nod to him. He smiles and nods back. He reaches the altar and stops by the GROOM.

RUGGIERO

You're late. Where have you been? Poor Claudia must have circled the church a thousand times. Now she'll be too dizzy to walk down the aisle.

FRANCESCO

That's the effect you have on her, Ruggiero. That's why she's marrying you.

FRANCESCO smiles then hugs the GROOM.

RUGGIERO

Don't try to soft-soap me, Francesco. Where's the ring?

FRANCESCO

Ring?

FRANCESCO anxiously searches his pockets.

RUGGIERO

Don't fool around, Francesco.

FRANCESCO LAUGHS as he pulls out the ring. PADRE PINO steps forward.

PADRE PINO

Gentlemen, please. The bride has arrived.

The WEDDING MARCH is heard and everybody stands. CLAUDIA, accompanied by her FATHER, walks slowly down the aisle.

CUT TO:

25 - EXT. CHURCH. DAY.

The ringing of BELLS. The doors open and the NEWLYWEDS emerge followed by their PARENTS, and FRIENDS. After the traditional congratulations and the customary throwing of confetti from all around him, RUGGIERO addresses them.

RUGGIERO

My friends. Make your way over to Franco's restaurant. There you can eat and be merry to your hearts content.

There is a loud CHEER, then the CROWD follow the NEWLYWEDS across the street to the bar.

FRANCESCO remains in the doorway of the church. He watches them all enter the garden at the back of the bar.

FRANCESCO feels a hand on his shoulder. He turns and faces PADRE PINO.

PADRE PINO

Not hungry, Francesco?

FRANCESCO

Yes. But I was just thinking of Ruggiero.

PADRE PINO

They make a lovely couple. Don't you think?

FRANCESCO

Yes they do.

PADRE PINO

Let's hope she keeps him out of trouble.

FRANCESCO

Padre, is it possible to meet someone for the first time and know she is the one?

PADRE PINO

Of course. Why have you had such an experience? I am told it's like been struck by a thunderbolt.

FRANCESCO

Yes, like a thunderbolt. You can't imagine how close that is to the truth.

(beat)

I'm sorry, I didn't mean to imply...

PADRE PINO LAUGHS.

PADRE PINO

That's okay. I wasn't always a priest. Now you run along and join the others.

FRANCESCO

Thank you Padre Pino. Thank you.

CUT TO:

26 - INT. CHURCH. DAY.

PADRE PINO enters. He closes the door.

PADRE PINO

Come, Lena. They have all gone.

LENA emerges out of a shadow. She kisses PADRE PINO'S hands.

PADRE PINO

You don't have to hide any longer, Lena.

LENA

Yes I do.

PADRE PINO

No, Lena. In the eyes of God we are all equal.

LENA

Try telling that to some of the people round here. They never forgive or forget.

PADRE PINO

God has forgiven you.

LENA

Maybe. But I haven't forgiven Him!

She pulls her scarf over her face and exits.

CUT TO:

27 - EXT. CHURCH. DAY.

LENA comes out and hurries along the street like a fugitive.

PADRE PINO watches after her. His attention is drawn to a MAN in a black shirt. The MAN is putting up a poster on the side of the church wall. PADRE PINO looks up to the sky, as if asking for guidance.

The MAN finishes then leaves. When the MAN is out of sight, PADRE PINO walks over to the poster. The poster is of Fascist propaganda. He rips it off the wall and screws it up.

CUT TO:

28 - EXT. BAR. GARDEN. NIGHT.

It is a warm Mediterranean night and the wedding party is in full swing. A BAND plays lively traditional music. Lights hung on trees and poles LIGHT UP the dance area. All around the dance area are small wooden tables.

FRANCESCO and a MAN – this is FRANCO MAZZA, sit at one of the tables. On the table there are a few empty bottles of wine. FRANCO is drunk. FRANCESCO watches the DANCERS.

FRANCO

I married when I was nineteen. Nineteen! Are you listening to me, Francesco?

FRANCESCO

Yes, I'm listening, Franco.

FRANCO

Yeah. Then what was I saying?

FRANCESCO

That you were a 19-year-old jerk when you got married.

FRANCO

Okay. It proves you were listening. Now where was I?

FRANCESCO

Look Franco. Every time you get drunk I hear the same old story. Why don't you go help your wife.

FRANCO looks over to the bar. He sees his WIFE serving the GUESTS. She seems rushed off her feet.

FRANCO

Victoria doesn't need help. She knows her place. You see she works and I drink. So tell me now, who is the jerk?

They both LAUGH. RUGGIERO joins them.

RUGGIERO

Glad to see my two good friends are having a great time.

FRANCO

Not as good as what's coming your way tonight, my dear Ruggiero. Tonight you find out what it's really for.

FRANCO LAUGHS. RUGGIERO and FRANCESCO exchange a glance.

RUGGIERO

Who is this? Is he with

you, Francesco?

(LAUGHTER)

You haven't told me why you

were late, Francesco?

CUT TO:

29 - INT. DE'ANDRIA MANSION. NIGHT.

The light on the landing outside MARIA'S room is on. She tiptoes in her socks past the half-open door of her mother's bedroom and pauses. She hears the ticking of the wall clock in the hall below and now the reassuring, soft snoring of her mother.

MARIA comes down the stairs into the hall. She approaches her father's study. The door is slightly open. She hears her father and Pacula talking. She listens for a while.

PACULA (o.s)

That is the final piece of the jigsaw. When do you expect him?

DON DE'ANDRIA (o.s)

Soon. Manno and Furio have gone to fetch him.

PACULA (o.s)

Soon the great railway will dance to your tune.

MARIA walks quietly past the study and down the hall. She stops by the door and pulls on her riding boots. And as MARIA opens the door to step out, ANNA confronts her.

ANNA

Where are you going?

MARIA

Please Anna, you must help me. I must go to him. I have to see him again.

ANNA

Looks like you've already made up your mind.

CUT TO:

30 - INT. STABLES. NIGHT.

As MARIA comes in and closes the door, a few horses watch from their stalls, ears pricked forward. She puts a finger up to her lips indicating for silence.

MARIA walks on. Her horse is in the last stall at the far end of the barn. She can see her horse BIANCO, his head erect and still, watching her all the way.

Then BIANCO whinnies as she comes up to the stall, putting his face forward for her to rub.

MARIA

Shush, Bianco! They'll hear you.

She reaches out for him and he lets her touch the velvet of his muzzle, but only briefly, tilting his head up and away from her.

MARIA

Stop, fooling around, Bianco. There's no time. We must hurry.

MARIA goes into the stall and takes off the horse's blanket. As she swings the saddle over him, he shifts away.

MARIA

Easy Bianco, easy.

She lightly fastens the girth and puts on the bridle. She leads him out of his stall.

CUT TO:

31 - EXT. STABLES. NIGHT.

MARIA leads the white horse out into the yard and quietly out of the gates. Then she mounts and looks across to the house.

MARIA
Be very quiet, Bianco.

MARIA rides the horse slowly toward the gate that leads into the woods. And as they reach the woods, she quickens the pace.

CUT TO:

32 - EXT. BAR. GARDEN. NIGHT.

An OLD MAN, bent under a huge accordion joins the band. He immediately launches into a spirited Can Can. The DANCERS begin kicking and bottom-shaking. Other GUESTS around the dance area clap.

RUGGIERO, FRANCESCO, and FRANCO are still at the table.

RUGGIERO
You've seen her the one time and already you're in love?

FRANCO
And you called me a jerk? Get outta here, Francesco!

RUGGIERO
What's got into you. Did that thunderbolt really hit the tree and not right there?

RUGGIERO lightly taps FRANCESCO'S head, gently pushing it.

FRANCESCO
If you'd been there, seen her, you would understand.

RUGGIERO LAUGHS.

RUGGIERO
This calls for a double celebration.

Come Francesco. You too Franco.

The THREE MEN slightly stagger to the bar.

CUT TO:

33 - INT. BAR. NIGHT.

The THREE MEN join a CROWD of GUESTS by the bar and mix in.
A YOUNG TEENAGE GIRL approaches FRANCESCO.

YOUNG TEENAGE GIRL

Francesco, here you are. How long must I wait to dance with you?

FRANCESCO

Lucia. I'm busy for the moment. Maybe later.

LUCIA shrugs then goes out to the garden. FRANCO turns to
FRANCESCO.

FRANCO

**Now that's whom you should be paying some attention to. Not
some strange woman you glimpsed for a few seconds.**

FRANCESCO

Strange woman!? Her name is Maria De'Andria.

On hearing the name, FRANCO'S eyes widen his mouth opens.

FRANCESCO

You know her?

FRANCO

**Her father has been trying to get his hands on this place for
months.**

FRANCESCO and FRANCO exchange a confused look. At this point RUGGIERO interrupts them.

RUGGIERO

C'mon you two, let's party. Why the long faces? What are you a couple of horses? Don't you get it; 'long faces', 'couple of horses'?

They all LAUGH.

CUT TO:

34 - EXT. BAR. GARDEN. NIGHT.

ON THE DANCE FLOOR. It is alive with the twirling movements of the dancers and the happy wheeze of the accordion.

The music changes, a YOUNG WOMAN sings a traditional love song. The dance area is cleared. Then as the BRIDE and her FATHER begin to dance the GUESTS around the dance floor CLAP. CUT TO:

35 - INT. BAR. NIGHT.

FRANCO is now behind the bar helping out. VICTORIA gently pushes him aside as she picks up the empty glasses off of the counter. FRANCESCO and RUGGIERO lean against the bar.

RUGGIERO

It won't work, Francesco. Listen to me. You know I love you like a brother.

(beat)

So be realistic. C'mon what have you got to offer her?

FRANCESCO

Plenty. I'm not going to stay in this town forever.

RUGGIERO

Yes, yes. I've heard that many times, 'when you go to America and make your fortune'.

FRANCO

(cuts in)

Besides, she wouldn't come here. She's a lady. And ladies don't give people like us a second glance.

FRANCESCO

Keep out of this, jerk!

On Franco's reference to a lady, VICTORIA reacts. She gives FRANCO a filthy look.

FRANCO

Victoria. How could you possibly think I meant you? I am deeply hurt.

VICTORIA

You're hurt? I get it. This the old 'hurts me more than it hurts you' routine. You men are all the same. Never tell the truth if a lie lets you sleep more easily.

FRANCO

Victoria, there are times when I think you are a perfect bitch.

VICTORIA

And what about the other times? Like when you want to jump on my bones, with your breath stinking of alcohol.

FRANCESCO and RUGGIERO LAUGH. VICTORIA looks away and serves. RUGGIERO'S MOTHER comes to the bar. She grabs RUGGIERO'S arm.

MOTHER

Come, Ruggiero. It's time to dance with your beautiful bride.

RUGGIERO

Okay, mama. Sorry fellas duty calls.

FRANCESCO watches RUGGIERO squeeze past the PEOPLE in the packed bar.

VOICE

Everybody. The bride and groom have taken the floor.

The GUESTS move out towards the garden and as the bar clears FRANCESCO suddenly stands and something makes his face light up.

FRANCESCO'S POV. MARIA stands in the doorway.

CUT TO:

36 - EXT. BAR. GARDEN. NIGHT.

The dance area is full. The GUESTS are generally enjoying themselves. FRANCESCO and MARIA are also dancing. As the music changes most of the people spill off the dance area.

FRANCESCO and MARIA along with other GUESTS form a ring around the dance area. An OLD COUPLE enter the ring and they dance the 'tarantella' while the GUESTS clap to the beat.

As FRANCESCO claps he looks to his side where MARIA is also clapping to the beat. He smiles.

FRANCESCO

You having a good time?

MARIA nods and smiles.
I'm so glad you made it.

MARIA

So am I.

SEVERAL COUPLES break through the human ring and join the OLD COUPLE. They dance the 'tarantella' too. FRANCESCO grabs MARIA'S arm.

FRANCESCO

C'mon.

FRANCESCO pulls her onto the dance floor. MARIA pulls back.

MARIA

I can't. I don't know how.

FRANCESCO

Neither do I.

It isn't long before MARIA picks up the dance steps. Not far from the dance area, PADRE PINO watches the DANCERS. As MARIA spins her eyes catch PADRE PINO watching her. Their eyes lock for a moment in recognition. PADRE PINO stares at her, ominously. CUT TO:

37 - INT. BAR. NIGHT.

The bar is empty. The SOUNDS of music and people having a good time can be heard from the garden. FRANCO comes out of the toilet and is just moving away to go out to the garden, when he feels a sharp prod in the crook of his back. He looks over his shoulder to see MANNO standing behind him. FURIO walks round and faces FRANCO. He speaks in a low voice.

FURIO

Don De'Andria would like the pleasure of your company. Let's

go.

FRANCO

What, now?

MANNO

Right now.

FRANCO

I can't leave now. I have a wedding going on.

MANNO

Then I will fire this gun in my pocket.

Trying not to attract too much attention FRANCO agrees to go.

FRANCO

In that case, you have

persuaded me.

As FRANCO gets his hat and coat, FURIO goes to the window and looks out.

FURIO'S POV: CROWDED dance floor, FRANCESCO spinning MARIA around. She is having a wonderful time. FURIO attracts MANNO'S attention. MANNO joins him by the window and looks out. He looks back to FURIO. They exchange a smile. FRANCO interrupts them.

FRANCO

Can we make this quick? As you can see I am very busy.

CUT TO:

38 - EXT. BAR. GARDEN. NIGHT.

As FRANCESCO escorts MARIA off the dance area his eyes briefly see FRANCO and the TWO MEN as they walk towards the square.

FRANCESCO looks puzzled for a moment then turns back to MARIA. PADRE PINO watches them with interest.

CUT TO:

39 - INT. DE'ANDRIA MANSION. STUDY. NIGHT.

RICARDO PACULA sits on a circular leather sofa. DON DE'ANDRIA pours two large brandies. He lights up a cigar.

DON DE'ANDRIA

I'm sure you will appreciate fine brandy, such as this. It was given to me by the minister of Spain, as a token of friendship.

DON DE'ANDRIA Walks over and gives the glass to PACULA who nods then takes a sip.

PACULA

It certainly is a fine brandy.

DON DE'ANDRIA takes his place behind his desk.

DON DE'ANDRIA
It's over 30 years old.

As DON DE'ANDRIA takes a sip there is a knock on the door.

Come.

The door opens and FURIO enters followed by FRANCO and MANNO.

DON DE'ANDRIA
Franco. Come and sit down.
A drink, Furio, for my friend.

FRANCO sits in a leather chair in front of the desk. FURIO brings him a drink.

FRANCO
Thank you.

DON DE'ANDRIA
Well, Franco. Do we have a deal?

FRANCO
I'm a little confused why you want my bar and land. There are many bars in Cosenza. Why mine?

PACULA
(cuts in)
Are you an imbecile? Luciano has offered you more than double what your property is worth. Now just say yes and you can go.

FRANCO gives PACULA a casual look then turns back to DON DE'ANDRIA.

FRANCO
Yes it is a kind and generous offer. But I couldn't possibly accept.

DON DE'ANDRIA
Why not?

FRANCO
Over the years I have worked very hard to build up my business. All that time I had hoped to eventually pass it on to my children, as my father did before me.

DON DE'ANDRIA
I hate defeat. You've dragged your heels on this matter for too long. The fact you made me bring you here by force I can forgive. Now you tell me you don't want to do business with me?

FRANCO
That's the strength of it.

DON DE'ANDRIA
That I will not forgive. So I have decided to ignore this feeble excuse. I am still prepared to buy you're property.

FRANCO
I don't think you understand me, Don De'Andria.

DON DE'ANDRIA bangs the table in anger.

DON DE'ANDRIA

No, Franco. You understand this. I'll have your property whether you sell it to me or not!

FRANCO

And how will you do that?

DON DE'ANDRIA stares at FRANCO, coldly.

CUT TO:

40 - EXT. COSENZA. SQUARE. NIGHT.

A CROWD of PEOPLE stands around a makeshift gaming casino in the middle of the square. Some watch, some gamble.

FRANCESCO and MARIA walk across the square. As they walk, FRANCESCO Occasionally notices the odd glance in his direction, from MARIA. He smiles at her.

She sees the makeshift casino.

MARIA

What are they doing there?

FRANCESCO

Losing money they've worked hard all week for.

A MAN from the CROWD shouts over to them.

MAN

Francesco!

FRANCESCO looks to the MAN. He ignores him and turns back to MARIA.

MARIA

That man is calling you, Francesco.

FRANCESCO

Yes I know. He's a loser. Let's go.

TONIO waves at them from his seat beside the roulette table and beckons them over to join him.

TONIO

Francesco! Come over here. Bring me some luck.   This wretched croupier is determined I shall not win tonight.

FRANCESCO

See? What did I tell you.

She puts an arm around his waist, pleading.

MARIA

Let's go over. It might be fun. Please.

FRANCESCO smiles.

FRANCESCO

Okay.

FRANCESCO and MARIA stop at the roulette table.

MARIA

Go on, Francesco. Have a go.

FRANCESCO

Okay. Move over Tonio and let me try. I've had nothing but good luck today.

He smiles at MARIA. She smiles back. FRANCESCO buys some chips then turns to MARIA.

FRANCESCO

Give me a number.

MARIA

Six. My lucky number.

FRANCESCO throws two chips onto the table and shouts out his choice to the CROUPIER.

As CROUPIER puts the chips on the six square, TONIO throws a couple chips down on the table.

TONIO

I'll have the same. I've got this feeling that our luck's going to be in tonight. Right Francesco? We share everything, eh?

TONIO grins as he eyes MARIA. FRANCESCO nudges TONIO'S stomach with his elbow.

FRANCESCO

What's the matter with you? Where's your manners?

TONIO'S grin turns to a sheepish smile then turns to see the CROUPIER spin the wheel. As if mesmerized, everyone's eyes follow the spin of the wheel as the little white ball bounces in and out of the numbered sockets, teasing first one number then another.

Gradually the wheel begins to slow and the movement of the ball becomes less frenetic. Then almost painfully the ball bobbles for the last time and comes reluctantly to rest.

CROUPIER

Nine!

TONIO

Shit! That's me cleaned out.

The CROUPIER claws in all the losing chips with his shovel, leaving just the winners on the table to be paid out. TONIO turns to FRANCESCO.

TONIO

She's not as lucky as you thought, eh?

FRANCESCO

Get lost, Tonio. Maybe it's your luck that stinks.

TONIO half-smiles and shrugs.

CUT TO:

41 - INT. DE'ANDRIA MANSION. NIGHT.

PACULA walks down a corridor. He stops outside MARIA'S room. He knocks. There is no reply. He knocks again.

PACULA

Maria my love. It is I, Ricardo.

Open the door.

The door does not open. But another door further down does. ANNA comes out.

ANNA

Maria is not feeling too good. She will not see anyone.

PACULA

I am not 'anyone', Anna. She will see her future husband.

He opens the door and enters. ANNA quickly disappears into her room. PACULA storms out.

CUT TO:

42 - EXT. COSENZA. SQUARE. NIGHT.

As FRANCESCO and MARIA walk away from the makeshift casino and cross the square to where the HORSES are tied, LENA comes out of the shadows. She approaches them.

LENA

Francesco. What a lovely evening. It compliments your young lady.

MARIA

Why thank you.

FRANCESCO

Yes it does.

LENA

Look after this girl, Francesco. She's too beautiful to be left alone.

LENA smiles then walks away. MARIA turns to FRANCESCO.

MARIA

What a charming woman. Who is she?

FRANCESCO

Er. Just a charming woman.

They stop by their HORSES and mount.

CUT TO:

43 - INT. DE'ANDRIA MANSION. STUDY. NIGHT.

DON DE'ANDRIA is pacing about the room. FURIO and MANNO watch him. Raising his hands up in despair DON DE'ANDRIA turns towards MANNO.

DON DE'ANDRIA

For his children! The man is an imbecile. He refuses to offer any reasonable explanation for this, this idiocy.

MANNO .

Give me the word and he'll no longer be a problem.

DON DE'ANDRIA

He's left me no choice. But you must use an outsider.

FURIO

I know the very man. His name is Puntina. He works as a guard at that prison in Reggio.

DON DE'ANDRIA

Is he reliable?

FURIO

Hundred percent. He's like a rock. He never talks. He listens and also has the gift of loosening tongues. Now tell me, can you not use a man like that?

DON DE'ANDRIA

Get him. I'm sure a widow with children to feed will be more reasonable.

At that moment PACULA bursts in.

PACULA

Maria. She's not in her room!

DON DE'ANDRIA'S eyes narrow. He looks at FURIO and then to MANNO.

DON DE'ANDRIA

Have you seen, Maria.

MANNO nods.

CUT TO:

44 - EXT. DE'ANDRIA MANSION. GATES. NIGHT.

FRANCESCO and MARIA ride quietly and stop at the gates.

MARIA

That's far enough. I must go on alone from here. Thank you for a wonderful evening.

FRANCESCO

When will I see you again?

MARIA

As soon as I can.

Suddenly, from behind the gates, FURIO and MANNO, appear with half a dozen capable looking MEN in black shirts, behind them. They surround FRANCESCO and MARIA.

FRANCESCO

What is this? What do you want?

DON DE'ANDRIA and PACULA appear. DON DE'ANDRIA hisses through his teeth.

DON DE'ANDRIA

Maria. Get down and come here.

MARIA

(shocked)

Papa. It's not what you think.

DON DE'ANDRIA doesn't wait for her to dismount. He moves forward and pulls her off the horse.

FRANCESCO

Hey! Don't take it out on her. It's not her fault.

FRANCESCO dismounts and is immediately on the receiving end of a torrent of abuse from PACULA.

PACULA

**You filthy peasant. How dare you
even think you are of the same
class as Maria! What have you
done to her?**

FRANCESCO

Not what you're thinking.

PACULA shakes his head, knowingly.

PACULA
But I hear you peasants do nothing else but breed like rabbits.

FRANCESCO
You've got a mind like a cesspool. You Fascist pig!

FRANCESCO loses his temper, moving forward as if to strike him. FURIO and MANNO grab FRANCESCO and hold him. The SIX BLACK SHIRTS move closer. At this moment PACULA spits in FRANCESCO'S face and LAUGHS.

MARIA breaks away from her father. She screams as she confronts them.

MARIA
How dare you! Let go of him!

PACULA
Keep out of this.

PACULA pushes her away. MARIA falls to the ground.

This is too much for FRANCESCO. Instinctively his fist lashes out, striking PACULA just above his chin and breaking his upper lip. There is a gush of blood as PACULA reels backwards.

The SIX BLACK SHIRTS help FURIO and MANNO wrestle FRANCESCO to the ground. They severely beat him until he is unconscious.

DON DE'ANDRIA steps forward and rolls FRANCESCO'S limp body over. He looks down at him. FRANCESCO stirs.

DON DE'ANDRIA
Kill him!

MARIA scurries across and throws herself across FRANCESCO.

MARIA
No, papa. Don't do this. I'll do
whatever you wish.

DON DE'ANDRIA looks down at her long and hard.

DON DE'ANDRIA
And you will never see him again?

MARIA
Yes! Yes!

MARIA'S eyes well. Tears stream down her face. PACULA, with one hand nursing his lip with a handkerchief, pulls MARIA to her feet with the other, and drags her through the gates. DON DE'ANDRIA turns to MANNO.

DON DE'ANDRIA
Put him on his horse. And if he ever shows his face here again,
kill him.

They throw FRANCESCO onto his horse. His body instantly flops over the horse. His arms hang down either side with the side of his face pressed hard against the horse's neck.

FRANCESCO opens a BLOODIED EYE and stares at DON DE'ANDRIA'S evil look. FURIO gives the horse a hard slap. The HORSE gallops away.

CUT TO:

45 - EXT. FRANCESCO'S HOME. NIGHT.

FRANCESCO'S horse stops. As he tries to dismount he falls off and hits the ground. He remains there. The HORSE whinnies.

A window nearby opens. LENA pokes her head out. She sees FRANCESCO struggling to get to his feet. She closes the window. In a few moments LENA is by FRANCESCO'S side.

CUT TO:

46 - INT. DE'ANDRIA MANSION. BEDROOM. NIGHT.

MAFALDA is still asleep. Suddenly she is startled awake by the bedroom door banging open and hitting the wall with a thud. MARIA falls into the room. She hits the floor.

DON DE'ANDRIA enters and immediately lays into his daughter, pulling and slapping her. MAFALDA jumps out of bed.

MAFALDA
Stop that, Luciano. What's happened?

DON DE'ANDRIA
What's happened? Your daughter has been with that peasant from Cosenza. That's what's happened!

MAFALDA
Leave her. I beg you. I'll talk to her.

DON DE'ANDRIA

I'll leave her. But first she deserves to be taught a lesson. So don't interfere!

DON DE'ANDRIA gives MAFALDA a sharp shove. She falls onto her bed.

CLOSE ON: MAFALDA'S anguished face, as we hear the sound of SLAPS.

MARIA (o.s)

Mama! Mama!

CUT TO:

47 - EXT. FRANCESCO'S HOME. NIGHT.

FRANCESCO sits on a bed with his back to the wall. LENA comes in from the kitchen. She carries a cup in one hand and a bowl of water in the other.

LENA

Those kind of people aren't for the likes of us. We mean **nothing to them** .

She hands him a hot drink. He takes it.

FRANCESCO

Maria is not like them. She's different. Nothing will keep us apart.

LENA dabs a cloth into the bowl. She then wrings it out and starts to clean the blood of his face.

LENA

Then you'll have to be more careful, Francesco.

(beat)

This cut above your eye looks nasty.

FRANCESCO winces then painfully forces a smile as LENA carefully cleans the cut.

FRANCESCO

On occasions like this I don't know what I'd do without you, Lena.

LENA

On occasions like this you need a nurse, not a wife.

LENA unrolls a bandage and proceeds to wrap it around FRANCESCO'S head.

FRANCESCO

My face must be in a right mess. I can't go out looking like this. What would people think?

LENA

If they see me coming out of here they'd think we'd had some kind of dispute.

FRANCESCO

Or think it happened in the height of passion?

FRANCESCO LAUGHS; having faced death a few hours before, he is now experiencing an enormous feeling of relief. LENA smiles, at the thought.

LENA

Go on, have your drink then get to sleep. I'll look in on you in the morning.

CUT TO:

48 - INT. MARIA'S BEDROOM. DAY.

MARIA paces back and forth. ANNA watches her.

MARIA

It is almost a week that I've been locked in here. I can't stand it no longer. Anna I need your help again. I must see him.

ANNA

I'm sorry, Maria. It's too dangerous. Not just for me but also for your Francesco. If you see him again you'll be as good as signing his death warrant.

SILENCE. Then she hears VOICES coming from the patio. MARIA goes to the window and looks out from behind the curtains.

CUT TO:

49 - EXT. DE'ANDRIA MANSION. PATIO. DAY.

A CAR is waits outside. DON DE'ANDRIA emerges from the house with PACULA. They climb into the car. The SIX BLACK SHIRTS are in another car behind. The two cars move off and make their way to the gates then disappear.

At the window the curtains go back further revealing a smiling MARIA.

CUT TO:

50 - INT. STABLES. DAY.

MARIA saddles BIANCO. She leads him out of the stall.

CUT TO:

51 - EXT. COSENZA. SQUARE. DAY.

The square is busy with PEOPLE buying various goods. There is a market in progress. MARIA rides into the square. She dismounts. Several PEOPLE give her an odd look then walk on.

LENA walks past MARIA. She carries a couple of bags full of groceries. MARIA notices her.

MARIA

Signora! Signora!

LENA stops. She turns and stares at MARIA.

Do you remember me? I was with Francesco in this very square.

LENA

Yes, I remember you. Come.

LENA turns and continues to walk. MARIA takes BIANCO'S reins and follows her.

CUT TO:

52 - INT. FRANCESCO'S HOME. DAY.

FRANCESCO is asleep on a bed. His bandages are off and his face is almost healed. He moans in his sleep.

FRANCESCO

(asleep)

No. Don't papa. Don't!

SIX GUNSHOTS are heard, simultaneously. As he awakes he springs to an upright position, still SCREAMING:

No!

At this moment MARIA enters. She sees him staring wildly and goes to him.

MARIA

What is wrong Francesco?

FRANCESCO

Nothing.

FRANCESCO looks at her then his anguish turns to joy.

Maria. How did you find me?

MARIA

Lena. She brought me to you.

FRANCESCO gently touches her hair.

FRANCESCO

You're an extraordinary woman.

MARIA in turn touches the faint scars on his face.

MARIA

Did they hurt you badly, my love?

FRANCESCO gently shakes his head.

FRANCESCO

You know, I said that for a woman like you a man would take on the world.

MARIA

Yes I know. Anna told me. And I'm so glad that 'man' was you.

FRANCESCO

How is it with your father? What would he say if he knew you were here?

MARIA places a finger on his lips.

MARIA

Shush. Let's not talk about that. This is our moment. Nothing else exists.

FRANCESCO looks at MARIA helplessly. A fierce resolve fills her face, looking at FRANCESCO with her innocent eyes as she begins unbuttoning the front of her dress. She lets it fall to the floor and steps out of it. She is wearing a green jersey underneath.

FRANCESCO is transfixed as the jersey rises, then recedes over her bare breasts. She looks into his eyes, warmly. He gently pulls her down. As they kiss she begins to pull off his clothes.

He kisses her on her eyes, her mouth, her neck, his hands cupping the soft roundness of her breasts'. She pushes him away gently and slips under the sheets. Their legs entwine, their hands explore eachother's bodies

They kiss tentatively, then warmly, then fiercely. They make love with a passion.

CUT TO:

53 - EXT. FRANCESCO'S HOME. DAY

LENA sits on a small wall, her legs crossed. She eats some bread and cheese. A MIDDLE-AGED MAN approaches her. He first looks from side to side then faces her.

> MIDDLE-AGED MAN
> **Well?**

She ignores him and looks the other way. He prods her shoulder. She turns back to him. He shows her the money. Then he wraps the money around his two fingers and simulates sexual intercourse, his fingers going in and out of the notes.

> LENA
> **That's right. Fuck your money! You see my legs? They're closed. Come back when they open.**

> MIDDLE-AGED MAN
> **Half-day closing, huh?**

MIDDLE-AGED MAN walks away, LAUGHING.

CUT TO:

54 - INT. FRANCESCO'S HOME. DAY.

FRANCESCO and MARIA lie on the bed facing eachother, with a look of satisfaction spread across both their faces.

> MARIA
> **Before I came in you screamed?**

> FRANCESCO
> **It was just a bad dream.**

MARIA

What about?

FRANCESCO

(reluctantly)

Nothing of importance.

MARIA

Tell me about yourself. Where are your parents?

FRANCESCO

Dead. My mother died a few years ago and my father died when I was twelve. I had an older brother. He too died when he was fifteen.

MARIA

Fifteen? How did he die?

FRANCESCO

He was murdered. Now that's enough about me let's talk about you.

MARIA

There's not a lot I can say; school, institutions, piano lessons, not many friends. As you can see I've had a boring existence.

(beat)

Until I met you.

FRANCESCO leans forward and kisses her lips. After a few moments she pulls away.

FRANCESCO

What's the matter?

MARIA

Soon I'll have to go back to Rome and finish my studies. I'm dreading it.

FRANCESCO

Why?

MARIA playfully pinches his chest and smiles innocently. He flinches and smiles.

MARIA

You know why.

FRANCESCO

(jokes)

Then take me with you. I'll make myself really small and jump into your top pocket next to your heart.

MARIA pinches him again, but a bit harder. He GIGGLES like a child.

MARIA

I'm serious. I don't want to go.

FRANCESCO

Then don't.

(beat)

Why don't we just run away. Leave everything behind us?

MARIA

(smiles)

Seems like our only option. But where would we go?

FRANCESCO

America. The land where dreams are made. I have some money
saved. And if I work my socks off for a few weeks we should
have enough to go.

MARIA

You would do all this for me?

FRANCESCO

I would die for you.

MARIA

No, my love. I want you alive.

MARIA puts her arms around him and pulls him in to her. They
kiss as if it's their last.

CUT TO:

55 - EXT. DE'ANDRIA MANSION. DAY.

MARIA gallops through the gates and stops by the stables.

CLOSE UP: WINDOW. Curtains draw back. PACULA stares out.

CUT TO:

56 - INT. DE'ANDRIA MANSION. HALL. DAY.

PACULA looks through the window. His POV: MARIA leads her
HORSE into the stables.

CUT TO:

57 - INT. MARIA'S ROOM. DAY.

MARIA is folding some clothes. She lays them on her bed. The door opens. ANNA enters.

ANNA

They've not long been back. I don't think they missed you. But you are really tempting providence!

MARIA

I don't care anymore, Anna. You just wouldn't believe what's happened to me.

ANNA looks at the clothes on the bed.

ANNA

Try me. You'd be surprised in what I'd believe.

CUT TO:

58 - EXT. MARIA'S ROOM. DAY.

PACULA stands by the door. He listens.

MARIA (o.s)

He as good as proposed marriage to me. In a few weeks we're going to run away together. To America.

PACULA has heard enough. He walks away and descends the stairs.

CUT TO:

59 - INT. DE'ANDRIA MANSION. STUDY. DAY.

DON DE'ANDRIA sits behind his desk. FURIO and MANNO stand facing him. Next to them is a HUGE MAN.

FURIO

This is Officer Puntina. He's the guard from the prison I

told you about.

DON DE'ANDRIA looks up at the man and acknowledges him. PUNTINA nods back, confidently. The door opens and PACULA enters. He walks over to DON DE'ANDRIA and whispers in his ear.

DON DE'ANDRIA'S eyes widen as he listens. PACULA finishes and stands upright.

DON DE'ANDRIA

There's been a change of plan, Mr Puntina. You will eliminate not one peasant but two. His name is Francesco Acciardi.

PUNTINA

Acciardi? That name rings a bell. Ten years ago there was an Acciardi on my wing. He allegedly took his life in his cell.

FURIO

It was Acciardi's father.

PUNTINA

The plot thickens.

PUNTINA looks at PACULA. PACULA looks away avoiding PUNTINA'S eyes. PUNTINA turns back to DON DE'ANDRIA.

This Francesco Acciardi, why kill him? Why not give him to me. I'll make him suffer for a while and then he'll follow in his father's footsteps, literally.

MANNO

But how do we get him into prison?

DON DE'ANDRIA

(smiles)

We frame him for the murder of Franco Mazza.

(beat)

Tell me Mr Puntina, you said Acciardi 'allegedly' took his own life?

PUNTINA

That's because he didn't take it. I did.

SILENCE. DON DE'ANDRIA gives him a puzzled look.

PUNTINA

You see, Acciardi was an ex-cop and ex-cops are the last people to have in your prison. He was uncontrollable.

DON DE'ANDRIA

Okay. But no fuck-ups!

CUT TO:

60 - INT. BROTHEL. NIGHT.

PUNTINA, and a WOMAN are in a bedroom. They are both naked, and lying on the bed. At the side of the bed, on a chair, a prison guard's uniform is neatly folded. PUNTINA gets up.

PUNTINA

Would you like a drink?

WOMAN

I don't mind. What time is it?

PUNTINA

Just before ten.

WOMAN

Do you have to be early in the morning?

PUNTINA

No. I go when it pleases me.

WOMAN

Lucky man.

PUNTINA

Glad you think so.

PUNTINA goes through a door to the next room. In a moment he returns to the bedroom holding a long thin cane.

PUNTINA

You're going to be lucky too. Get up.

WOMAN

What's the matter with you?

PUNTINA

Get up.

He stands there, flexing the thin cane.

WOMAN

I'm too tired to play games. Come to bed.

Quite suddenly, he lashes out. The cane strikes her arm. She gives a cry.

WOMAN
Ow! That hurt!

PUNTINA
Get up.

She sits up in the bed, staring at him.

WOMAN
I think I need that drink.

PUNTINA
You bitch.

PUNTINA strikes her across the legs with the cane, cutting into her flesh. She screams. She touches the cut on her leg.

PUNTINA stands over her, enjoying himself. There is a drop of perspiration on his forehead. He breaths a little heavier as he holds the cane poised.

WOMAN
You're mad.

She jumps up, panic-stricken. PUNTINA lays into her with the cane, slashing and hitting her. She screams and tries to cover herself, but without success.

One blow catches her across the right breast, leaving a thin red line, with some blood seeping through, and she shrieks.

For one wild moment she tries to grab at the cane but PUNTINA just pushes her against the wall and LAUGHS. Again PUNTINA hits her. She runs for the door.

PUNTINA

Don't you enjoy it?

The WOMAN is like an animal at bay, shaking, terrified, her hair straggling down, perspiration on her body, and those vicious marks where the cane has caught her, on her face, on her breast, on the arms.

WOMAN

Please don't. Why are you doing this?

PUNTINA

If they want to be loved, I love them.
If they are whores I beat them.
(beat)
To death.

She grabs a bottle from the table and throws it at him. It hits PUNTINA, cutting his forehead. He LAUGHS.

She runs to the window and tries to rip open the curtains. But PUNTINA is right behind her, and lays into her back.

Again and again, the cane comes down lashing thin welts into her flesh. Once more she screams. Then SILENCE.

PUNTINA raises the cane. It is bloodstained.

CUT TO:

61 - EXT. DE'ANDRIA MANSION. NIGHT.

The light from MARIA'S bedroom shines bright. FRANCESCO climbs over the wall. He crosses in the darkness to the house. He climbs up the stones that jut out from the wall. He reaches Maria's window.

He looks in. His POV: MARIA sits in a comfy chair reading a book. He taps gently on the window. She sees him and comes to open the window. He climbs in.

CUT TO:

62 - INT. FRANCO'S BAR. NIGHT.

FRANCO is behind the bar. The place is empty except for one drunken OLD MAN. The OLD MAN is asleep with his head facing down on the table.

FRANCO

Peppino its time for you to go. I need to lock up. Hey Peppino!

PEPPINO doesn't react. FRANCO walks over and shakes PEPPINO'S shoulder.

FRANCO

C'mon, Peppino time to go home.

PEPPINO wakes up. FRANCO helps him up.

CUT TO:

63 - EXT. FRANCO'S BAR. NIGHT.

From across the street, PUNTINA watches the bar. PEPPINO staggers out and the door closes. PEPPINO slides down the wall and falls asleep.

CUT TO:

64 - INT. FRANCO'S BAR. NIGHT.

FRANCO closes the door. He goes back behind the bar and with a wet cloth he wipes the counter top. The opening of the door startles FRANCO. PUNTINA enters and stops at the bar.

FRANCO

Sorry, friend but I'm closed for the evening. I open again in the morning.

PUNTINA

Wrong. You're closed. Period!

PUNTINA pulls out a gun and shoots FRANCO twice in the chest and once in the neck. The force of the bullets flings FRANCO back against the shelves. Glasses crash to the floor.

As FRANCO falls he drags the shelf full of stacked glasses down with him. PUNTINA puts the gun back in his jacket makes the sign of the cross.

PUNTINA walks round the counter and removes a wristwatch from FRANCO'S limp arm then goes to the till and empties it. He walks out calmly closing the door behind him.

CUT TO:

65 - EXT. FRANCO'S BAR. NIGHT.

PUNTINA steps out. He turns quickly and steps on PEPPINO. PEPPINO stirs. PUNTINA hurries away. PEPPINO awakes and just catches a glimpse of the back of PUNTINA as he rounds a corner. PEPPINO climbs to his feet and staggers back into the bar.

CUT TO:

65A - INT. FRANCO'S BAR. NIGHT.

PEPPINO

**Franco! Franco! I need
another drink.**

PEPPINO stops at the bar counter. His POV: shelf hanging down; glasses smashed then FRANCO on the floor behind the bar. At once he sobers up and hurries round the counter. FRANCO, bleeding from the neck wound, makes small GURGLING noises.

PEPPINO

Franco, what happened?

Who did this to you?

FRANCO'S hand slowly comes up. His finger points to the door. He tries to speak but his words come out half strangled.

FRANCO

Assassin!

PEPPINO

Don't try to speak. I'll get help.

PEPPINO exits. FRANCO coughs blood. His eyes close.

CUT TO:

66 - INT. FRANCESCO'S HOUSE. DAY.

FRANCESCO is asleep on his bed. Suddenly the door bursts open and in seconds the room is full of POLICEMEN.

Startled awake, FRANCESCO jumps out of bed straight into the arms of two BURLEY POLICEMEN. They handcuff him. GARGIULO – chief of police, confronts him.

FRANCESCO

What the fuck is going on?

GARGIULO

You're under arrest for the murder of Franco Mazza.

FRANCESCO

What! Franco's dead? There must be some mistake.

GARGIULO

No mistake! Stop play acting we have witnesses who saw you running away from the bar.

FRANCESCO

Who are these witnesses? They're lying!

LENA pushes her way through the POLICEMEN. GARGIULO crosses to a jacket hanging on the door. He puts his hand in the pocket and pulls out a wristwatch. He thrusts the wristwatch under FRANCESCO'S nose.

GARGIULO

If they are liars then what does
this make you? Found in your jacket.
Get him out of here.

FRANCESCO stares at the wristwatch in confused SILENCE. LENA bites her closed fist.

LENA

What are you doing to him? Take
your filthy hands off him!

TWO POLICEMEN restrain her. GARGIULO turns to her.

GARGIULO

Calm yourself, whore or I'll

pull you in too.

LENA

Whore am I? That's not what you

usually call me.

The POLICEMEN holding LENA try hard to hold back their laughter. GARGIULO gives them an angry look.

GARGIULO

Get her out of here!

CUT TO:

67 - INT. POLICE STATION. CELL. DAY.

FRANCESCO is on a wooden bed. He stares up at the ceiling. The SOUND of keys grating in a lock. He turns his head to the door. It opens. PADRE PINO enters. FRANCESCO sits up.

PADRE PINO

What is going on, Francesco. You are accused of robbing and

murdering Franco Mazza. God rest his soul.

FRANCESCO

I didn't do it, Padre Pino.

PADRE PINO

Then who did?

FRANCESCO

I don't know. Sometimes he could be a pain in the ass. But no one hated him enough to kill him.

PADRE PINO

When was the last time you saw him?

FRANCESCO

The night of Ruggiero's wedding.

PADRE PINO

You had his wristwatch. His widow swears that Franco had it with him Yet you tell me you haven't seen him for over a week. How can that be?

FRANCESCO

I don't know.

(beat)

Wait a minute. Now I remember. On the night of the wedding. Franco told me that Don Luciano De'Andria was after his bar.

PADRE PINO

Don De'Andria?

FRANCESCO

(nods)

Then that same evening I saw Franco leave the bar with two of De'Andria's men. Maybe he refused to sell and they killed him.

PADRE PINO

That still doesn't explain the watch.

FRANCESCO

What about if Gargiulo is on De'Andria's payroll?

PADRE PINO

Tell me, Francesco, did he know that his daughter was with you at the wedding?

FRANCESCO

Yes.

PADRE PINO stares at him in SILENCE.

CUT TO:

68 - INT. MARIA'S BEDROOM. DAY.

ANNA is helping MARIA dress. The door opens and DON DE'ANDRIA enters. He opens a wardrobe and grabs several dresses and throws them to the floor.

DON DE'ANDRIA

Start packing!

MARIA

Why? Are you throwing me out?

DON DE'ANDRIA

And where would you go? To your little peasant. I don't think so. At this moment he's in jail for murder.

MARIA

What are you saying, papa?

DON DE'ANDRIA

Last night your peasant murdered a close friend of his for money.

MARIA

That cannot be. He couldn't have done it.

DON DE'ANDRIA

There are witnesses!

MARIA

They lie!! He was with me all night!

DON DE'ANDRIA'S eyes go wide and about to pop out of their sockets. The door opens again and MAFALDA enters.

MAFALDA

What is all this screaming for?

MARIA

Mama. Francesco has been accused of murder. But he didn't do it. He was with me last night. You must take me to the police. I will tell them.

DON DE'ANDRIA reacts swiftly. He slaps MARIA across the face, knocking her to the floor. He turns to ANNA.

DON DE'ANDRIA

Now pack this whore's bags immediately.We're all leaving together. And if by chance she gets away from you again I'll have you both killed. Do you understand?

ANNA nods. MARIA sobs in her mother's arms.

CUT TO:

69 - INT. POLICE STATION. CELL. DAY.

PADRE PINO stands by the cell door. FRANCESCO sits on the side of the bed.

FRANCESCO

I can't tell you where I was last night.

PADRE PINO

You don't have to.

(beat)

Protecting a lady's honor, eh? You really were struck by the thunderbolt. Let's hope her love is as strong as yours.

FRANCESCO

It is, Padre.

PADRE PINO

Then she'll come forward and tell the truth.

SILENCE. Door opens and PADRE PINO exits.

CUT TO:

70 - CLOSE ON: LENA'S FACE: eyes misted over.

PULL BACK:

71 - INT. COURTROOM. DAY.

LENA'S POV: two GUARDS lead FRANCESCO, in chains, into the CROWDED courthouse.

A LAWYER sifts through some papers on a desk opposite the bench. FRANCESCO and the GUARDS stop by him. The GUARD leaves them.

FRANCESCO

You my lawyer?

MAZZARI

Yes. Stefano MAZZARI.

FRANCESCO

I'm innocent.

MAZZARI

Yes, yes. Of course. But it's not me you need to convince.

VOICE

All rise.

The courtroom rises as the JUDGE PIRLO enters.

CUT TO:

72 - EXT. DE'ANDRIA MANSION. DAY.

A SERVANT is explaining to PADRE PINO.

SERVANT

They left last night.

PADRE PINO

Where have they gone?

SERVANT
I don't know

PADRE PINO
When are they expected back?

SERVANT
Going by how many cases they packed, not for a long time.

PADRE PINO
I see. Let me get this straight. They've gone away for a long time and they never told you where.
SERVANT
That's correct.

PADRE PINO
What if you have a problem?

SERVANT
We never have a problem.

PADRE PINO grabs him and wrestles him to the floor and sits on him.

PADRE PINO
Then what is this then! Now tell me where they've gone or so help me I'll forget I'm a priest.

The SERVANT struggles but PADRE PINO has him well pinned down. He gives up.

SERVANT
They've gone to Reggio. They have a villa there by the sea.

CUT TO:

73 - INT. COURTROOM. DAY.

FEDERICO MORANDI – prosecution, paces up and down in front of the jury. He is in the middle of his opening speech.

MORANDI

Frank Mazza was a good honest man. Murdered by a man he had helped countless times. A man he regarded as a friend. A Judas, that robbed and brutally murdered him.

MORANDI looks to FRANCESCO.

Ladies and gentlemen of the jury, today I will prove that FrancescoAcciardi is that 'Judas'.

MORANDI sits down. STEFANO MAZZARI stands and walks over to the jury. He claps, mockingly.

MAZZARI

A very impressive story. And that's all it is, a story. Not the truth but a possibility.

(beat)

We will try to prove otherwise.

CUT TO:

74 - EXT. TRAIN STATION. DAY

The TRAIN chuffs off, the red light on the final carriage disappears round the bend in the cutting through the forest; the steam and smoke climb into the clear blue skies beyond.

CUT TO:

75 - INT. TRAIN. DAY

MOVING. The corridors are crowded, mainly SOLDIERS.

PADRE PINO sits by a window. He looks across the rough geography of bough and leaf, to the village and the station, just visible through the trees.

CUT TO:

76 - INT. COURTROOM. DAY.

FRANCESCO is seated next to STEFANO MAZZARI. TWO GUARDS sit behind them. FRANCESCO looks across to LENA who is about fifteen feet away, in the courtroom pews. He half-smiles at her. She smiles back at him. A little further along are RUGGIERO and, his wife.

MORANDI is in the middle of questioning a WITNESS.

MORANDI

Mr. Mori, you say you heard three shots?

MORI

That is correct.

MORANDI

And immediately after you saw a man come out of the victims bar?

MORI

Yes.

MORANDI

Is that man in this court?

MORI

Yes. He is Francesco Acciardi.

MORI points an accusing finger at FRANCESCO. There is uproar in the court. FRANCESCO jumps to his feet.

FRANCESCO

Liar!!

The GUARDS force FRANCESCO back into his seat. The JUDGE hits the top of the bench with his gavel.

JUDGE

Order! Order! I will not tolerate this kind of behavior in my court.

The court settles down. MORANDI continues.

MORANDI

So, Mr Mori, you are certain the defendant murdered Franco Mazza in cold blood?

STEFANO MAZZARI stands.

STEFANO MAZZARI

Objection! Mr Mori only saw my client come out, not commit the crime.

JUDGE PIRLO looks at MAZZARI.

JUDGE PIRLO

So does the defense concede that your client was at the scene of the crime?

STEFANO MAZZARI

According to Mr Mori my client was there. So yes I must agree. But he never saw my client shoot the victim.

MAZZARI sits down. FRANCESCO turns to him

FRANCESCO

What are you saying? I wasn't there!

STEFANO MAZZARI

Trust me. I know what I'm doing.

FRANCESCO

I'd rather trust a snake.

MORANDI

(to MORI)

No further questions.

JUDGE PIRLO looks at MAZZARI.

MAZZARI

I have no questions at this moment.

(to FRANCESCO)

There's no point in questioning him. He clearly saw you.

FRANCESCO grabs MAZZARI'S arm, firmly.

FRANCESCO

Who's put you up to this?!

MAZZARI breaks loose. The GUARDS move closer.

MAZZARI

Refrain yourself.

JUDGE (o.s)

The witness may step down.

CUT TO:

77 - EXT. REGGIO CALABRIA. RAILWAY STATION. DAY.

PADRE PINO climbs into a horse drawn carriage. He gives the COACHMAN instructions and in a few moments they are gone.

CUT TO:

78 - EXT. VILLA DE'ANDRIA. DAY.

The villa overlooks the sea giving a beautiful view. The horsedrawn carriage comes into view. PADRE PINO steps out and pays the COACHMAN.

PADRE PINO knocks on the door. The door opens and FURIO stands there. As he sees the priest his mouth opens in surprise.

FURIO

Padre Pino. What are you doing here?

PADRE PINO

I've come to see, Don Luciano.

PADRE PINO doesn't wait to be invited in.

Excuse me.

He moves past FURIO. FURIO'S mouth opens again.

CUT TO:

79 - INT. COURTROOM. DAY.

The second witness, SANTE SUMMA, is now in the witness box.

SUMMA

The murderer ran straight into me. He had the look of the devil in his eyes.

MORANDI

So you got a good look at him?

SUMMA

Of course. It was him!

He too points an accusing finger at FRANCESCO. Again there is uproar.

CUT TO:

80 - EXT. VILLA DE'ANDRIA. BALCONY. DAY.

PADRE PINO and DON DE'ANDRIA are in conversation.

DON DE'ANDRIA

Yes. Mr Mazza came to my home. He begged my help. Apparently he was in financial distress. He was one of life's losers. He offered his bar and land as collateral's.

PADRE PINO

And did you help him?

DON DE'ANDRIA

Of course. I gave him the value of his property. Obviously his assassin got an early Christmas gift.

PADRE PINO

I made some inquiries and I learned of some interesting facts about the new line from Reggio to Rome. Funny enough it runs straight through Franco Mazza's land.

(beat)

Did you know that?

DON DE'ANDRIA'S eyes narrow.

DON DE'ANDRIA

No. But thank you for bringing it to my attention.

PADRE PINO

I have a train to catch. I'm sorry for the intrusion. Goodbye.

CUT TO:

81 - INT. COURTROOM. DAY.

GARGIULO, Chief of Police, is now in the witness box.

GARGIULO

I found the victim's wristwatch in the defendant's jacket. Of course he denied all knowledge of it.

MORANDI

Thank you. No further questions.

JUDGE PIRLO looks to MAZZARI.

JUDGE PIRLO

Would you like to cross-examine the witness?

MAZZARI shakes his head. RUGGIERO jumps to his feet.

RUGGIERO

That bastard wouldn't cross the street without someone paying him!!

JUDGE PIRLO

How dare you interrupt this court! Sit down or I'll hold you in contempt. The witness may step down.

RUGGIERO sits back down. FRANCESCO looks at him and half smiles. RUGGIERO shrugs. GARGIULO leaves the witness box. MORANDI approaches the bench.

MORANDI

Your honor in view of the evidence and that the defense do not respond it is evident that their client is guilty. The defendant has no alibi.

LENA steps forward.

LENA

Yes he has. He was with me all night.

CUT TO:

82 - INT. COURTROOM. DAY.

BACK OF THE COURT. PACULA enters and quietly walks down the aisle. He moves into a pew and sits just behind the GUARDS watching FRANCESCO. JUDGE PIRLO sees him. He gives PACULA a confident smile.

MORANDI looks at a list then looks at LENA then to MARRAZI.

MORANDI

If this woman is one of your witnesses I don't appear to have her name on my list. This is highly irregular.

MARRAZI

She is not my witness. I've never set eyes on her before now.

JUDGE PIRLO
(to GUARDS)
Remove that woman.

SOUNDS of amazement and despair are heard in the court. FRANCESCO jumps to his feet.

FRANCESCO

This is not a trial. This is a farce! I am innocent!

SILENCE. Then the court erupts. There is uproar. JUDGE PIRLO brings down his gavel several times on the bench. MORANDI turns to PACULA and smiles triumphantly.

JUDGE PIRLO

Order! Order!

(SILENCE)

A further disturbance in my court and I will have no option but to clear it!

FRANCESCO

I am innocent I tell you!

JUDGE PIRLO

Sit down, Mr Acciardi. You'll have your chance to speak.

DISSOLVE TO:

83 - INT. COURTROOM. DAY.

FRANCESCO is on the stand. He is in the middle of his testimony. MAZZARI stands before him.

FRANCESCO

And he left the wedding with two men who I believe work for Don De'Andria.

MAZZARI

And did you find anything odd about that?

FRANCESCO

Franco looked distressed. Besides he would never have left a wedding on his own accord.

(beat)

I'm certain what happened to him was a result of that meeting with Don De'Andria.

JUDGE PIRLO looks at PACULA who gives him a cold stare. Then he looks at MORANDI. MORANDI stands.

MORANDI

Objection! The court is not interested in Mr Acciardi's assumptions.

JUDGE PIRLO

Objection sustained. The witness will stick to answering questions and not coming to his own conclusions.

MAZZARI

Thank you, Mr Acciardi. No further questions.

MAZZARI sits down.

DISSOLVE TO:

84 - INT. COURTROOM. DAY

MORANDI is in the middle of cross-examining FRANCESCO.

MORANDI

I'm told, Mr. Acciardi, that your father was a fine police officer. And many years ago you had thought of joining the force too.

RUGGIERO springs up.

RUGGIERO

Yes! And he would have made a fine policeman. And an honest one!

CLAUDIA pulls him back down to his seat. JUDGE PIRLO shoots him a look. MORANDI turns back to FRANCESCO.

MORANDI

And I'm sure he would have!

(to FRANCESCO)

Tell me. This is not the first time murder has entered your life, is it?

FRANCESCO'S eyes widen. He remains SILENT.

Your father shot and killed a man in cold blood. He emptied his pistol in the victim's head. Six shots!

Once again the court erupts. PACULA smiles. PEOPLE talk amongst themselves.

MORANDI(cont.)

And isn't it also true that the reason you never joined the force is because your father disgraced the uniform?

FRANCESCO'S despair is turning into a boiling RAGE.

FRANCESCO

Yes! Yes! He hung himself in his cell. Is that what you wanted to hear?!?

MORANDI

Is that what led you into a life of crime?

The three GUARDS ready themselves. But FRANCESCO'S rage builds and builds until he is almost berserk.

FRANCESCO

You bastard! What led you into a life of crime! What led Don De'Andria into a life of crime? Ask him why he's framing me! What led the judge into a life of crime?! Ask him why he's part of this farce.

JUDGE PIRLO

Mr Acciardi! Calm yourself.

FRANCESCO

Everybody in this court knows I am innocent!

There is UPROAR in the court. JUDGE PIRLO is SLAMMING his gavel vigorously. The GUARDS move in. MORANDI continues to intimidate FRANCESCO.

MORANDI

(grins)

Acciardi, you're losing it. Is this what happened with Franco Mazza?

FRANCESCO

Losing it?!

LENA SHOUTS shaking her head, but is not heard: drowned by the NOISE.

FRANCESCO explodes. He grabs MORANDI and pulls him across the witness box. The GUARDS struggle to free MORANDI.

LENA'S FACE, white with shock, amid the UPROAR she faints.

GUARDS try to drag FRANCESCO out but he holds firm.

FRANCESCO

Who the fuck do they think they are!? You judges? Your courts! Your lawyers! Your establishment!

(CALMS)

I'll escape and I'll kill you all. That I promise.

CUT TO:

85 - EXT. THE YARD. MORNING.

FRANCESCO sits on a bench looking across the busy yard.

Two MEN look to be having a disagreement over something. FIRST CON – this is ANGELO, shoves the other and the incident breaks into a fight. Other CONS gather around watching them rolling about on the ground; punching, kicking, biting. FRANCESCO stands and walks towards the fracas.

For a moment ANGELO manages to shove him to one side and together they roll across the ground. Blood from the SECOND CON'S cut is streaming over ANGELO'S face, mixing with that from his own scratch marks, and from a nasty gash which has opened up under his left eye. In the ensuing struggle the SECOND CON reaches down and pulls something out from under the turn-up of his trousers.

FRANCESCO

Look out! He's got a knife!

The SECOND CON holds the blade in his right hand as he throws himself at ANGELO once more.

ANGELO clutches the SECOND CON'S wrist, and for a moment it seems that the SECOND CON is winning. The knife is edging ever nearer to ANGELO'S throat. Then with a final desperate effort, ANGELO twists the SECOND CON'S wrist and slowly but reluctantly the knife wobbles and falls to the ground.

FRANCESCO rushes over and kicks it out of the SECOND CON'S reach. The two MEN brake apart and slowly rise to their feet. And seeing the GUARDS moving towards them decide not to continue.

The CON wipes away the blood, which is still dripping from his lips. He spits out blood.

SECOND CON

It's over for now. Another day, eh?

With the SECOND CON gone, FRANCESCO turns to ANGELO.

FRANCESCO

Jesus, that guy's a loony. He could have killed you. Did you see the look in his eyes? Do you believe all that stuff about revenge?

ANGELO

No, it is just a pathetic attempt to frighten me
(smiles)
Welcome to hell. I'm Angelo.

CUT TO:

86 - INT. CELL BLOCK. DAY.

FRANCESCO walks down the corridor to his cell.

VOICE

Acciardi!

FRANCESCO turns. PUNTINA stands there, legs straddled wide, hands on his hips, his club swinging idly at his side. His jaw is stuck out arrogantly. He beckons FRANCESCO over with his finger.

FRANCESCO hesitates. Then he walks over to him. INMATES file into their cells, all keeping a watchful eye on the situation that is about to develop. FRANCESCO stops in front of PUNTINA. PUNTINA looks at FRANCESCO a long moment.

PUNTINA

Acciardi?

FRANCESCO

Yes, sir.

PUNTINA

What happened out in the yard?

(SILENCE)

I didn't get your answer, Acciardi.

FRANCESCO

It's because I didn't give one

PUNTINA

Smart ass, eh? You see this, Acciardi?

PUNTINA lifts up his club.

This club does my talking whenever I run into this kind of
attitude. You think you're harder than this?

SILENCE, FRANCESCO remains calm.

PUNTINA

No I didn't think so. You peasants
Are all the same; cowards.

On this last inference, PUNTINA prods FRANCESCO'S chest with
the club. FRANCESCO steps back slightly; trembling with rage.

PUNTINA

I knew another peasant who was also a coward; Franco Mazza.

FRANCESCO

What do you know about Franco?

PUNTINA

Just that you were both close.

(beat)

How would you like to get closer to him?

PUNTINA leans forward and speaks almost to a WHISPER.

PUNTINA

I can arrange it. I'll do you the
same favour I did, Mazza.

FRANCESCO

You?

PUNTINA
He died like a coward.

FRANCESCO
(SHOUTS)
You fuck!!

PUNTINA reacts swiftly. His hand flies out in a wide arc and cracks FRANCESCO across the face! With the other hand he swings his club heavily toward FRANCESCO'S skull.

FRANCESCO grabs at it and rushes PUNTINA, In a second, the two men are on the floor tussling for the weapon.

THREE GUARDS come running at them.

The INMATES SHOUT and JEER abuse at them from their cells as the THREE GUARDS move in on FRANCESCO who is now on top of PUNTINA, pushing down on the club locked against PUNTINA'S windpipe.

The THREE GUARDS claw and beat and finally manage to pull FRANCESCO'S grip loose. PUNTINA lies there on the floor, CHOKING and GASPING for breath.

TWO of the GUARDS hold FRANCESCO'S arms pinioned behind him. SILENCE except for PUNTINA'S GAGGING noises. Slowly he pulls himself up and glares at FRANCESCO.

While the TWO GUARDS hold FRANCESCO, the THIRD GUARD wrenches FRANCESCO'S head back by the hair and holds that position. PUNTINA starts the beating; methodically. Slowly at first. A punch to the gut. A club on the kidneys. A kick in the shins. A club to the rib cage. A kick in the groin. He quickens the pace.

Then, the THIRD GUARD lets go of FRANCESCO'S hair, FRANCESCO'S headsprings forward only to meet A full-blooded blow in the face from the club.

FRANCESCO'S entire face and body is a MASS of BLOOD. He passes out. But still PUNTINA - SWEATING and BREATHING heavily - keeps the blows coming with deadly accuracy. Bones start to CRACK, BRUISES cut open.

The THREE GUARDS exchange a look. Then another GUARD – this is ZANETTI, appears. He steps in.

ZANETTI

That's enough.

PUNTINA ignores him and continues to beat FRANCESCO'S limp body.

ZANETTI

(SHOUTING)

That's enough, Puntina!

(to the

THREE GUARDS)

Get him the fuck out of here!

THREE GUARDS obey. They pull FRANCESCO'S limp body back. Out of PUNTINA'S reach.

PUNTINA stands there, PANTING and SWEATING profusely. His shirt and pants are totally spattered with BLOODSTAINS. He looks with satisfaction at FRANCESCO'S BLOODIED and broken carcass.

PUNTINA
Like I said I'm here to
correct the wrong attitudes!
Take him to the box!

CUT TO:

87 - INT. PRISON. CORRIDOR. DAY.
As PUNTINA saunters past the row of cells on the tier he pulls out a handkerchief and slowly wipes the end of the BLOODSTAINED club. CONS watch him in silence from their cells.

A CON – this is RUSSO, with his hands gripping the bars of his cell door, stares out at PUNTINA, blankly.

PUNTINA swings his club, rapping RUSSO'S knuckles, viciously. RUSSO recoils!

PUNTINA
Who're you looking at, scum!

CUT TO:

88 - INT. PRISON. THE BOX. DAY.
The THREE GUARDS enter and dump FRANCESCO'S limp body on a table. FRANCESCO is still.
CUT TO:

89 - INT. PRISON. THE BOX. AFTERNOON.

DOCTOR walks in. He is met by VINCI. He points to the table.

VINCI

He's over there, Doc.

DOCTOR heads towards the table. FRANCESCO lies inert on it. DOCTOR looks at him almost incredulously for a moment, then shoots VINCI a questioning look?

VINCI

(flatly)

Puntina.

DOCTOR

Who else but that sadistic maniac would inflict such mutilation.

DOCTOR starts the examination.

DOCTOR (cont.)

He'll live. But for how long. I wouldn't like to guess.

CUT TO:

<u>90 – INT. THE BOX. CELL 6. AFTERNOON.</u>

The cell is 8 foot by 8 foot and devoid of anything except the steel ceiling, the walls, and the concrete floor. The DOOR swings opens.

TWO GUARDS dump FRANCESCO'S still-unconscious body into the cell. Then they strip him naked. The TWO GUARDS exit slamming the steel door shut leaving FRANCESCO in almost total DARKNESS.

CUT TO:

<u>91 – INT. PRISON. GOVERNOR'S OFFICE. EVENING.</u>

DOCTOR is protesting to PERICARDI, governor of the prison.

DOCTOR

That man should be in the infirmary. Not in that stinking lice and roaches' den!

PERICARDI

He attacked a guard and has got to accept the punishment for that action. And as for the few bruises well that is expected. Officer Puntina acted only in self-defense.

DOCTOR

Self-defense? A few bruises? He was beaten to a bloody pulp for God's sakes. Hasn't he suffered enough?!

Phone RINGS. PERICARDI snatches up the handset.
PERICARDI

Yes! Oh hi, honey – Yes I got our reservation, best seats in the house - look, can I call you back? I have someone with me. – No it's not that important – No. honey it's not more important than you, I'll phone you back – Yes, yes, I love you too!

PERICARDI hangs up. He coughs and turns back to the DOCTOR.
PERICARDI

Now if there isn't anything else I'm a very busy man?

DOCTOR

Yes. That I can see.

DOCTOR turns and as he heads for the door, adds:
DOCTOR

He needs medical attention, yet he's locked up like a wild animal to sleep in his own shit and piss! He'll die and you know it!

He exits closing the door behind him. As PERICARDI reaches for the phone he SHOUTS after the DOCTOR.

PERICARDI

And if he don't he'll come out a better man! With a better attitude! And you'll still have the only job an incompetent doctor could get!

CUT TO:

92 - INT. THE BOX. EXT - CELL 6. NIGHT.

The BOX GUARD passes by cell 6 and hesitates. He sighs. Then he opens the peephole. His face screws up and his hand automatically goes to his nose. He pinches it.

CUT TO:

93 - INT. THE BOX. INT - CELL 6. NIGHT.

SIMULATED DARKNESS: A tiny AURA of LIGHT barely illuminates the peephole in the door making the cell a shade less than completely dark.

CUT TO:

94 - INT. THE BOX. EXT CELL 6. NIGHT.

BOX GUARDS POV: Through the PEEPHOLE faint image of FRANCESCO'S body on the cell floor.

He pulls away from the door and moves quickly down the corridor.

CUT TO:

95 - INT. THE BOX, INT - CELL 6. NIGHT.

SIMULATED DARKNESS: PEEPHOLE still open. Ray of light still shines in. And still FRANCESCO lies motionless.

MUFFLED CRACK of THUNDER somewhere in the distance. Then quick FOOTSTEPS from outside. Then KEYS GRATING in the lock. The door flings open and the light half fills the cell lighting FRANCESCO'S still body. In the doorway stand VINCI and OFFICER ZANETTI.

VINCI

I tell you, Zanetti. He's dead. You can smell it. Deadmeat!

ZANETTI stops by FRANCESCO'S limp body, and crosses himself. As he leans over the still body, FRANCESCO regains consciousness.

FRANCESCO'S POV: blurred vision of OFFICER ZANETTI.

FRANCESCO
(GROANING)

Puntina!!

FRANCESCO grabs at OFFICER ZANETTI clawing at him. GIGLI helps ZANETTI to restrain him. Then FRANCESCO grabs at him too.

ZANETTI

Take it easy. Easy.

ZANETTI easily breaks free. Another GUARD comes in and moves in to help but ZANETTI waves him back then SIGHS as he looks down at FRANCESCO.

ZANETTI

He's out again.

FADE TO:

96 - EXT. VILLA DE'ANDRIA. BEACH. DAY.

MARIA sits watching the waves rolling in from the sea. She is in deep thought. ANNA approaches and sits beside her.

ANNA

You must come now, Maria. We are packed and ready to go back to Cosenza.

MARIA

Did you see him?

ANNA

I tried but they said he wouldn't be seeing anyone for a long time. He's in solitary.

MARIA'S face contorts. Her hand instantly closes to a fist and comes up to her mouth. She bites her knuckle.

FADE TO:

97 - TO COMPLETE DARKNESS

FAINT animal-like GROWLS of fear and frustration fill the BLACKNESS. The SOUND of SLUSHING movements - as a pair of hands would make if moving back and forth on a wet, rough concrete floor - begin to overlap the previous SOUND.

FAINT FOOTSTEPS and something being DRAGGED grows LOUDER and LOUDER with each second - these two SOUNDS should be made obvious that they are coming from somewhere completely different from each other.

The close SOUND of SLUSHING movements starts again, but now mixing in with the distant FOOTSTEPS and DRAGGING.

Followed by a LOUD ECHOING CLANG. A six inch by six-inch SQUARE opens - it is a PEEPHOLE; the LIGHT from the PEEPHOLE is like a SHAFT of PALE GOLD illuminating the darkness.

In a brief moment we see the back view of FRANCESCO. He is NAKED and just about stands facing the LIGHT with an arm up to shield his eyes. A CLANGING metal to metal as a NOZZLE comes through the peephole.

FRANCESCO'S FACE is badly SCARRED; scraggy hair runs down over a scraggly beard. His EYES squint as his arm goes down. His MOUTH opens revealing BLOODIED TEETH and BLEEDING GUMS. He stands there; defiantly.

The NOZZLE EXPLODES. WATER gushes out at FRANCESCO with such a force that it literally lifts and batters him against the wall.

FADE TO:

98 - EXT. PRISON. THE YARD. MORNING.
The SUN rises hot and glaring in a CLOUDLESS SKY.

The general POPULATION goes about their business doing their various chores.

CUT TO:

99 - INT. THE BOX. INT - CELL 6. NIGHT.
SIMULATED DARKNESS: FRANCESCO'S FACE. His eyes are closed. His awkward pile of torso and limbs are still.

The BLOOD caking and drying on his WOUNDS. He is SWEATING. The SWEAT, mingles with the BLOOD, forming sticky little pools under and around his BODY. The LICE, greedily sensing a new host, hop over and around FRANCESCO, They begin industriously burrowing their way into his flesh. The ROACHES too make a cursory examination, then begin crawling over his NAKED BODY searching for something to eat.

FRANCESCO'S EYES open slightly. As he lies there, his senses adapting to this state of pseudo blindness. He GROANS softly, and attempts to sit up. He GROANS LOUDER and passes out again.

                                                                    DISSOLVE TO:

100 - INT. THE BOX. INT - CELL 6. NIGHT.
FRANCESCO MOANS and stirs slightly. He opens his eyes. Once again he tries to sit up. He GROANS again. This time he manages.

Slowly FRANCESCO becomes aware of SOUNDS: the faintest CHIRPING of a BIRD somewhere outside; the MUFFLED ECHO of some movement inside the building. His nostrils twitch. His hand flops to the floor. He feels a gooey substance and brings his hand up to examine it.

FRANCESCO'S HAND is covered in a mixture of BLOOD and EXCREMENT. His stomach heaves.

FRANCESCO tenses, then GROANS again clutching at his right leg with his soiled hands. Very slowly and carefully, FRANCESCO places one fist on the floor for leverage. With the other used as a balancer, he begins to exert pressure on his legs and upper torso.

FRANCESCO manages to lift himself up to a forty-five degree angle, and then, gently, he continues the action until he is standing. FRANCESCO stands still, swaying slightly. Then taking care to do everything in slow motion, he shifts his weight from one foot to the other and begins dragging himself in this shuffling method around the cell. He slaps his thighs.

FRANCESCO

(MUTTERS)

Come on, you lazy bastards, get moving!

FRANCESCO shuffles along in an ever-increasing arc until he feels the wall. He cautiously gropes his way along the surface. The steel surface is WET from the dankness of the weather outside.

FRANCESCO makes his way over to the LIGHT, which faintly surrounds the six-inch square peephole. He stands against the door.

FRANCESCO slowly revolves his tongue over his cracked and BLOODSTAINED LIPS. The SOUND of FOOTSTEPS ECHOING down the corridor outside. He tenses. MUFFLED tone of a voice, then a SCRAPING sound. He steps back from the door.

The PEEPHOLE opens. A full RAY of LIGHT brightens the door area.

VOICE

Here.

A HAND extends two slices of bread and a cup of water through the peephole. FRANCESCO hobbles forward and accepts the ration.

104

The PEEPHOLE is slammed but it does not shut; it springs back a little, allowing a thin ray of LIGHT. FRANCESCO opens his scummy fist in the LIGHT: his FINGERS are wet with his own waste.

FRANCESCO brings the cup to his lips. His hand is trembling slightly. He SIPS a few drops. He waits a moment then SIPS a little more. FRANCESCO leans against the wall, then he bites into the bread.

DISSOLVE TO:

101 - INT. PRISON. THE BOX. INT - CELL 6. MID-DAY.

FOOTSTEPS approaching again outside. The PEEPHOLE opens again.

VOICE

Gimme the cup.

FRANCESCO hobbles to the door. Gritting his teeth, he manages to lift the cup high enough for the HAND at the peephole to take. The HAND pulls the cup out.

FRANCESCO

Hey. How long have I been in here?

VOICE

Ten days.

The PEEPHOLE slams shut. SIMULATED DARKNESS: With his FINGER FRANCESCO writes on the wall, by the door, ten strokes in EXCREMENT.

CUT TO:

102 - INT. PRISON. THE BOX. EXT CELL 6.

A BOX GUARD - a PUNTINA type - This is DELAGO looks through the PEEPHOLE. FRANCESCO stands there. His chest and face are blotched in his own waste. He stares back, defiantly.

DISSOLVE TO:

103 - INT. PRISON. THE BOX. INT - CELL 6.

SIMULATED DARKNESS: FRANCESCO squats in a far corner of the cell. His body convulses! The cramps continue to wrack him! Finally, too exhausted to move, he collapses beside the little pile of excrement, and lapses into unconsciousness.

CUT TO:

104 - INT. PRISON. THE BOX. EXT-CELL 6.

DELAGO and a GUARD stand outside cell 6.

> DELAGO
> **Three? I could knock him out with two.**

> GUARD
> **You're on, Delago.**

> DELAGO
> **You'd better be ready to pay up.**

DELAGO unlocks the cell as quietly as possible. He withdraws his club and tiptoes in.

GUARD'S POV: through the open cell door he sees FRANCESCO asleep. DELAGO stepping over the piles of excrement. BANG!

BANG! - the club meets with FRANCESCO'S skull. The first BLOW awakes FRANCESCO and the second renders him unconscious.

DELAGO LAUGHS as he comes out. His hand stretched out. He takes the MONEY from the GUARD.
DISSOLVE TO:

105 - INT. PRISON. THE BOX. CORRIDOR.

DELAGO moves about the tier as QUIETLY as possible. Unrolling a two-inch thick canvas hose, he drags its length to the door of cell 6. Ever so gently, he undoes the peephole and peers in.

Through the peephole we see FRANCESCO. He is still prostrate near the pile of waste.

DELAGO grins. He places the nozzle of the hose into the peephole; then he signals the OTHER BOX GUARD waiting by the tap.

CUT TO:

106 - INT. PRISON. THE BOX. INT - CELL 6.

The WATER comes gushing out of the NOZZLE. It hits FRANCESCO so hard it throws his body against the wall. He scrambles to his feet and tries best he can to avoid the steady POUNDING of WATER, but the aim is true - the WATER follows FRANCESCO wherever he runs. Every time he tries to get to the forward area of the cell, DELAGO directs a steady blast at him!

FRANCESCO is hurled backward - crashing to the floor! He lies there - battered and exhausted. DELAGO CHUCKLES.

CUT TO:

107 - INT. PRISON. THE BOX. EXT - CELL 6.

DELAGO signals to his COLLEAGUE at the other end of tier. Then the canvas hose flattens.

A little TRENCH, which runs parallel to the cell, rows. WATER and the RESIDUE of FRANCESCO'S waste seeps out from under the STEEL DOOR and falls into the TRENCH.

FADE TO:

108 - INT. PRISON. THE BOX. INT - CELL 6.

With his fingers wet in excrement, FRANCESCO scratches his scraggly BEARD. Then a long hard scratch through his long scraggly hair, almost tearing it out by the roots. His mouth opens revealing BLOODIED TEETH and BLEEDING GUMS.

He turns to the steel WALL by the DOOR. TWENTY-SEVEN strokes of DRIED EXCREMENT STAINS: which have been put there daily by the only means he has, his own waste, are on the wall -the only one of the four steel walls at which the bath-time hose couldn't direct its fierce jet of water.

FRANCESCO'S FINGER marks a fresh stroke alongside the others.

He sits back; it is time for him to begin his daily "checking himself" ritual. Starting with his TOES, he feels his way up toward his groin. He GRUNTS with satisfaction as his soiled FINGERS come to a SCAB, Then a SOFT WOUND; it is SWOLLEN. He presses it gently and winces, then almost without emotion he diligently squeezes the PUS out. He grimaces.

CUT TO:

109 - EXT. PRISON CHAPEL. EVENING.

A strong WIND HOWLS across the yard. CONS hurry across the yard, their feet kicking up DUST only for the WIND to swirl it up at them.

The Chapel entrance is almost jammed with CONS trying to squeeze past each other - the FORCE of the WIND makes it virtually impossible to form any kind of queue. An ORGAN begins to PLAY a traditional CHRISTMAS CAROL.
DISSOLVE TO:

110 - TOTAL DARKNESS.

In the DARKNESS, a small figure appears. He is swimming TOWARDS US, With every stroke of his arm, he pushes back the BLACKNESS behind him, turning it into WATER, until all the BLACKNESS turns to WATER.

Then we see his FACE - it is FRANCO MAZZA - he is SCREAMING.

FRANCO'S VOICE
Help me.

A giant WATERFALL is pounding down on him. He swims frantically. But the more he moves his arms the further away he gets.

DISSOLVE TO:

111 - INT. PRISON. THE BOX. INT - CELL 6.

SIMULATED DARKNESS: FRANCESCO wakes with a start! FRANCO'S VOICE echoing in his head:
FRANCO'S VOICE

Help me! Please help me!

FRANCO'S VOICE echoes repeatedly, until FRANCESCO can't stand it any more. The VOICE now changes to that of a YOUNG BOY.

YOUNG BOY

Why did you leave me, Francesco?

He covers his ears but still hears the VOICE.

FRANCESCO

I Had to! I was scared! I was scared!!

The PEEPHOLE flings open and the shaft of LIGHT falls on FRANCESCO'S NAKED body. He is sitting in a corner with his chin between his knees and his hands covering his ears.

FRANCESCO

(MURMURING)

Leave me alone. Leave me alone. I am dead too.

The PEEPHOLE. DELAGO peers in.

CUT TO:

112 - INT. PRISON. THE BOX. GUARDS QUARTERS. NIGHT.

OFFICER GIGLI and OFFICER ZANETTI are resting when DELAGO hurries in.

DELAGO

Acciardi's goin' bananas. He's talking to his own shit.

(CHUCKLES)

Won't be long now before the 'white coats' pay him a visit.

DELAGO LAUGHS. OFFICERS' GIGLI and ZANETTI remain SILENT.

CUT TO:

113 - INT. PRISON. THE BOX. INT - CELL 6. NIGHT.

SIMULATED DARKNESS: FRANCESCO slowly paces around his cell. He stops and looks up.

FRANCESCO

Help me, God. You know, even when I was on trial for my life, I never once cursed You. I always believed You got reasons for making me go through this. Please God, show me the way.

He tries to take a step forward but manages only half a step then crumbles to the floor. Convulsing, while shudders of pain ripple over his emaciated body, he GASPS for breath; writhing and MOANING, He blacks out.

DISSOLVE TO:

114 – INT. HOUSE. EVENING.

DREAM SEQUENCE: A small BOY is sitting on a kind-faced WOMAN'S lap, Another BOY, much older than the other one, stands next to them. They all watch a MAN in a police uniform. He is making a WOODEN TOY HORSE. A log fire GLOWS in a grate, behind the MAN, illuminating and bathing him in an orange aura.

WOMAN

(to BOY

on lap)

You see what Papa is making for you, Francesco? Your very own horse.

LITTLE FRANCESCO
What about Mino, Mama?

MAMA hesitates. Then.

MAMA
**No. Your brother, Mino won't be
needing anything.**

PAPA finishes whittling the wood.

PAPA
There you are, Francesco.

MAMA squeezes FRANCESCO close.

MAMA
Isn't he a beauty. And he's all yours.

FRANCESCO turns to MINO.

LITTLE FRANCESCO
What about you, Mino?

MINO stares at him. SILENCE. Then MINO'S FACE begins to age, rapidly. FRANCESCO SCREAMS.

DISSOLVE TO:

<u>115 - INT. PRISON. THE BOX. INT - CELL 6. NIGHT.</u>
SIMULATED DARKNESS: FRANCESCO awakes SCREAMING:

FRANCESCO
No! You never got old! You weren't given a chance to, Mino?

FRANCESCO sits up, MURMURING; deliriously.

You never made it.

(beat)

God took you from me and then he took papa then mama. And now my Maria. That's all God has ever done; is take from me.

SILENCE. Then FRANCESCO'S EYES widen. Too weak to get up or shout, he slumps back to the floor. He blacks out again.

DISSOLVE TO:

116 - EXT. FIELD. DAY.

SECOND DREAM SEQUENCE: MINO runs down a hill, into the sunlit field and then through a forest. YOUNG FRANCESCO is close behind, crashing through the bushes, and branches. YOUNG FRANCESCO is LAUGHING. MINO is LAUGHING too. MINO reaches a cave. As he runs for the entrance he runs straight into a MAN.

YOUNG FRANCESCO finally reaches the cave and stops abruptly when he sees the MAN holding his struggling brother, MINO.

The MAN is in dirty torn clothing and looks like he hasn't shaven or washed in months. He has white hair and he looks angry. The MAN shouts at MINO. His voice makes YOUNG FRANCESCO jump.

MAN

What do you two think you're doing?

MINO

Get your hands off me!

MAN

Come on! Answer me, boy!

MINO
None of your business.

YOUNG FRANCESCO
You've got no right being here. This is private property.

The MAN yells, glancing round at YOUNG FRANCESCO. He spits as he shouts.

MAN
Don't you talk to me like that, boy!
(beat)
Private property, is it? And who is going to kick me off?

The MAN thumps himself in the chest with one finger.

MAN
Well, let me tell you something, boy, no one is going to kick me off. Because all I have in front of me is two little worms.

MINO
My father is a policeman.

The MAN looks down at MINO. MINO trembles.

MAN
Is he? Good! I hate policemen.

The MAN drags MINO with him. MINO starts crying and tries to break away, struggling weakly.

YOUNG FRANCESCO
Leave him!

YOUNG FRANCESCO looks through his tears at MINO, being dragged away into the cave. He follows them in.

CUT TO:

117 - INT. CAVES. DAY.

The MAN drags MINO in. YOUNG FRANCESCO follows at a distance.

YOUNG FRANCESCO
Where are you taking him?

The MAN stops, whirls MINO round and holds him against his chest. He looks at YOUNG FRANCESCO.

MAN
Come here!

MINO looks from him to his brother.

MINO
Run Francesco, run. Save yourself.

The MAN throws MINO to the ground.

MAN
Take off those trousers!

MINO shakes his head. YOUNG FRANCESCO starts to SOB.

The MAN leans over MINO and punches him in the face. MINO goes limp. The MAN looks back at YOUNG FRANCESCO, his eyes are wide and staring.

MAN
You! You; just stay there! Stay there, d'you hear?

YOUNG FRANCESCO stumbles backwards, almost falling; he has to turn to stop himself falling. He runs out of the cave.

CUT TO:

118 - EXT. FOREST. DAY.

YOUNG FRANCESCO races away through the woods, tears on his face, SOBBING hysterically, the breath whistling and whooping in and out of him; branches lash at his face.

CUT TO:

119 - EXT. CAVE. DAY.

YOUNG FRANCESCO is on the back of a WHITE HORSE holding tightly to a UNIFORMED MAN – this is his father; DEMETRIO ACCIARDI.   They jump down and make for the entrance. DEMETRIO pulls out a gun. They enter.

CUT TO:

120 - INT. CAVES. DAY.

The man is moving up and down over MINO. He has one hand over MINO'S LIFELESS face, clamped tightly over his nose and mouth.

DEMETRIO runs up behind the MAN, thrusting his pistol to the back of the MAN'S head. The pistol EXPLODES simultaneously; six times.

The MAN falls like a dead weight, flopping onto his side, then rolling forward onto his face. There is BLOOD leaking from the back of the DEAD MAN'S head, beneath the WHITE hair.

DEMETRIO falls to his knees by his dead son. He picks him up and cradles him. TEARS roll down his cheeks. He looks up at YOUNG FRANCESCO.

DEMETRIO

You should never have left him!

END SECOND DREAM SEQUENCE.

121 - BLACK SCREEN.

FRANCESCO (o.s)

I should never have left him, papa. I should never have left him.

FADE IN:

122 - INT. PRISON. THE BOX. INT - CELL 6. NIGHT.

FRANCESCO springs to an upright sitting position. And weak as he is, his eyes widen. His body tenses.

FRANCESCO

(MURMERS)

I was twelve, papa. Weak and frightened out of my skin. I regretted leaving Mino ever since. But you also left us, papa.

(SHOUTS)

You left us too, papa!

FADE TO:

123 - EXT. DE'ANDRIA MANSION. GARDEN. EVENING.

It is a hot evening. The PARTY is already in full swing, with a SEVERAL GUESTS milling around in the garden.

A CHEF looks up from the meat he is grilling on a barbecue pit as PADRE PINO approaches.

CHEF
Hello, Padre.

CHEF flips over a big steak then slides it on to a china plate. He hands it to PADRE PINO and points to a plate with various dressings.

PADRE PINO
(smiles)
Thank you.

As PADRE PINO helps himself to the dressing, he sees PUNTINA, and PACULA in deep conversation by the make-shift bar on the other side of the garden. PERICARDI and a few other GUESTS join him around the barbecue. They all acknowledge each other.

PERICARDI
How goes it, Padre?

PADRE PINO
Fine. I don't believe we've met?

PERICARDI
**Pericardi, Luca Pericardi. Governor
of Reggio prison.**
(beat)
**I hear the happy couple are
finally going to tie the knot.**

PADRE PINO
Yes. It seems that way.
(beat)
Try the meat it's delicious.

CUT TO:

124 - EXT. DE'ANDRIA MANSION. GARDEN BAR. EVENING.

PUNTINA leans against the bar as PACULA leaves him. A WOMAN walks over and stands next to PUNTINA. He looks at her and smiles. She returns the smile.

CUT TO:

125`- EXT. DE'ANDRIA MANSION. GARDEN. EVENING.

PADRE PINO'S POV: the other side of the garden; PUNTINA and the WOMAN LAUGHING together. He turns to PERICARDI.

PADRE PINO

What's Puntina doing here?

PERICARDI

He came along with me. Why,
do you know him?

PADRE PINO

I remember him from ten years ago.Puntina was the only witness at Demetrio Acciardi's inquest.

PERICARDI'S smile fades as PADRE PINO'S eyes lock with PUNTINA for a moment. PACULA joins them.

PACULA

(smiles)

Padre Pino. I am so glad you could come. I must apologize on behalf of my lovely Maria. She won't be joining us. She is not too good.

PADRE PINO

**Maybe it is I who should be apologizing. It seems everytime
I come she is not well.**

PACULA'S smile fades.

Up at Maria's bedroom window the curtains pull back.

CUT TO:

126 - INT. MARIA'S BEDROOM. EVENING.

MARIA stands by the window looking through the glass. Tears roll
down her cheeks.

DISSOLVE TO:

127 - EXT. DE'ANDRIA MANSION. GARDEN. EVENING.

PADRE PINO is with PERICARDI, and DON DE'ANDRIA by the
long buffet table. They help themselves to some food as they talk.

PADRE PINO

**It is there, unmistakable, in the eyes of every prisoner, a look:
haunted, hunted, controlled, yet boiling with rage just below
the surface.**

PERICARDI

Sure Padre. Maybe so. But it won't happen in my prison.

DON DE'ANDRIA slowly shakes his head.

PADRE PINO

**But surely it's the leaders among the population who help keep
the peace.**

DON DE'ANDRIA

Look Padre, I know you mean well but you don't understand. If you bend even the slightest, they'll figure you for a mark and you'll be caught up in something you'll regret later on.

PERICARDI

You shouldn't confuse loyalty with desperation.

PADRE PINO

No, it is you that is confused. These men serve their time because, for now, they choose to. What if someday they choose not to?

PADRE PINO breaks briefly, then as PERICARDI is about to give an answer, PADRE PINO cuts him off:

PADRE PINO

What if all at once these isolated outbursts became one all-powerful and united thrust?

PERICARDI is speechless. DON DE'ANDRIA answers for him.

DON DE'ANDRIA

(smirking)

But they won't will they Padre? Not if you and Luca have anything to do with it. You see, Padre, in one respect, you both do the same kinda work.

PADRE PINO watches DON DE'ANDRIA'S eyes widen; almost exploding.

You both instill the fear of God into them.

SILENCE.

FADE OUT:

128 - EXT. PRISON. THE YARD. DAY.

GENERAL POPULATION busy themselves in their various activities - exercising, playing soccer etc.

CUT TO:

129 - INT. INFIRMARY BUILDING. DAY.

MOVING. Two guards: ZANNETI and GIGLI, are closely followed by two prison trustees: RUSSO and CHIESA. RUSSO is carrying the front end of a folded up hospital stretcher, CHIESA carries the rear.

ZANNETI

My bet's he don't make it.

GIGLI

(WHEEZING

heavily)

It'll be you who won't make it if you don't slow down a little. What's the rush?

ZANNETI grins. They reach the end of the tunnel and leave the building.

CUT TO:

130 - EXT. INFIRMARY BUILDING. TUNNEL. DAY.

MOVING. Crossing over to a fifteen-foot high iron gate, the FOUR MEN stop. A GUARD is on duty. He nods then unlocks the gate. The four MEN pass through the gate.

CUT TO:

131 - EXT. YARD. DAY

MOVING. The TWO OFFICERS and TWO TRUSTEES move across

the yard.

ZANNETI looks over the yard. Some CONS are talking to each other. Some are fooling around. The rest pass a football around.

CUT TO:

132 - EXT. THE YARD. DAY.

MOVING. ZANNETI and GIGLI, and the two trustees RUSSO and CHIESA cross over to a square three-story building which is nestled against the far corner of the yard. This is the box: twenty strip cells - the most feared form of punishment the inmates have to deal with.

ZANNETI

What do you think Russo? Is it a safe bet?

RUSSO

I ain't never been locked up in there but I hear one week is enough to kill ya'. Acciardi's been in there 90 days now, right?

ZANNETI nods. RUSSO shakes his head ruefully.

RUSSO

I'd say Gigli here better keep his money in his pocket. More than likely it's a dead man we'll, be carrying outta there.

An armed GUARD looks down at them from the turret atop the forty-foot-tall concrete wall. They reach the steel entrance door of the box. ZANNETI RAPS on it with his club.

The eye-level meshed and barred six-inch square peephole in the door opens. A face with a long beaky nose under a set of shifty eyes appears. Assured he knows the visitors, the guard with the shifty eyes unlocks the door and lets them in.

CUT TO:

133 - INT. PRISON. THE BOX. DAY.

VINCI the officer in charge at the box meets the four men.

VINCI

Acciardi?

ZANNETI

Yeah.

VINCI jerks his thumb toward the far end of the corridor.

VINCI

Number six.

GIGLI

Right.

VINCI points to the stretcher.

VINCI

Maybe you should have brought a shroud along with it.

CUT TO:

134 - INT. CORRIDOR OUTSIDE STRIP CELLS. DAY.

As they walk down the corridor, RUSSO looks about furtively, his face screws up as his nostrils take in an awful smell: a combination of filth, and shit and piss. His hand goes to his face covering his mouth and nose. GIGLI notices RUSSO'S reaction.

GIGLI

What did you expect down here, the scent of roses!

They stop outside cell number six, ZANNETI pauses. He indicates to the two trustees.

ZANNETI

You better get that stretcher ready.

GIGLI opens the iron mesh peephole in the door and peers into the darkness of the cell. Suddenly he gasps.

GIGLI'S EYES widen; staring in disbelief.

TWO EYES are staring back at him out of the darkness.

ZANNETI turns the key in the lock. The cell door swings open.

SILENCE. FRANCESCO ACCIARDI hobbles out. He is naked and dirty. His skin is a mass of pus sores. Blood-caked scabs are crusted and scaly on his head and face; intermixing with his scraggy beard and matted hair. He slowly leaves the cell and stands, blinking slightly through red-rimmed eyes. He sways slightly, and then begins inching his way forward. Not really walking; extending one foot in front of the other dragging himself ahead moving slowly forward.

ZANNETI and GIGLI stand there speechless, amazed at what they are witnessing. RUSSO looks at CHIESA. They both grin; proudly, then shake hands.
FADE TO:

135 - INT. LENA'S HOUSE. MORNING.

LENA is dusting an old wooden cabinet. Black and white photographs rest on it. She looks at one of the photos: it is of her wedding day. In front of the photo there is a half-used candle. She lights it.

LENA looks at her image of when she was so young and beautiful and the handsome young man she had married. She SIGHS. Tears are forming in her eyes. She kisses the photo gently then diligently wipes it with the duster.

LENA puts on her coat and picks up a bag then exits.

CUT TO:

136 - INT. MESS HALL. DAY.

PUNTINA is on duty. He strolls about casually, eyeing everything around him meticulously, with one hand rubbing gently on the butt of his club.

ANGELO, and a few CONS sit at a table listening to RUSSO and CHIESA. RUSSO pushes aside his empty plate and a proud smile spreads across his face.

RUSSO

You had to see it to believe it, He was in that shit-hole 90 days 90 fucking days. No one's ever done that!

CHIESA

But Francesco walked out of there like it was nothing. You could have knocked them hacks over with a feather, they was so surprised.

ANGELO

Shame that motherfucker, Puntina wasn't there to see it.

ANGELO looks over to PUNTINA but when PUNTINA catches his eye ANGELO looks away.

ANGELO

What about that creep, 'if I don't break ya, the box will', Vinci?

RUSSO

Vinci, he didn't know whether to shit or turn purple!

LAUGHTER.

CUT TO:

137 - INT. PRISON. FRANCESCO'S CELL. DAY

The peephole opens and a GUARD looks in.

GUARD

Acciardi, you have a visitor.

He unlocks the door and motions to FRANCESCO to follow him.
CUT TO:

138 - INT. PRISON. VISITING ROOM. DAY.

LENA is seated at a table. As FRANCESCO enters she looks up and smiles. Tears form in her eyes.

FRANCESCO crosses to the table and Sits down opposite her. He reaches across the table and gently holds her hands. There is a GUARD in the corner of the room.

FRANCESCO
(softly)

Lena.

LENA looks at him pitifully.

LENA

How are you?

FRANCESCO

(half-smiles)

How is anyone in a place like this?

He pauses and WHISPERS softly:

FRANCESCO

Have you heard from Maria?

LENA

Yes.

FRANCESCO

(expectantly)

Well.

LENA

It's not good. She's getting married next week.

FRANCESCO stares at her in disbelief and slowly shakes his head.

FRANCESCO

She gave up on me.

LENA

No, Francesco. She hasn't given up on you. None of us have. She is being forced to marry that Fascist pig!

SILENCE.

FADE TO:

139 - EXT. PRISON. YARD. DAY.

The POPULATION stand around. From LOUDSPEAKERS strategically positioned in each corner of the yard they hear a radio broadcast.

ANNOUNCER

We are going directly to Venice Square. Where our Duce is about to address the nation.

There is quite a bit of frequency interference then the distinctive voice of BENITO MUSSOLINI, booms out.

Italians!!!

The POPULATION freeze. All attention is directed at the LOUDSPEAKERS.

CUT TO:

140 - EXT. PALACE OF VENICE. BALCONY. DAY.

On the balcony stands IL DUCE and other OFFICIALS.

DUCE

Soldiers, sailors and airmen! Black Shirts of the revolution and legions! Men and women of Italy! Listen to me!!!

CUT TO:

141 - EXT. COSENZA SQUARE. DAY.

The square is CROWDED with anxious villagers. PADRE PINO is also there, outside his empty church. LENA is not far away. They all listen intently to the broadcast.

DUCE (o.s)

People of Italy! Pick up your arms and remonstrate your tenacity, your courage, and your true value! We shall be victorious!!!

CUT TO:

142 - EXT. PALACE OF VENICE. SQUARE. DAY.

The massive CROWD go wild in agreement, cheering IL DUCE'S speech.

CUT TO:

143 - RAPID MONTAGE.

Newspaper headlines, newsreel footage, etc. etc., All reporting the start of World War 2.

DISSOLVE TO:

144 - INT. AIR RAID SHELTER. NIGHT.

The shelter is crowded. The distant sound of EXPLODING BOMBS. PEOPLE nervously exchange glances, anticipating the enemy bombs that might land above them.

CUT TO:

145 - EXT. STREET. NIGHT.

The distant sound of EXPLODING BOMBS.

CLOSE UP: FRANCO'S OLD BAR is now called 'MORI BAR'. It EXPLODES, suffering a direct hit.

CUT TO:

146 - INT. LENA'S HOME. NIGHT.

LENA and a CLIENT are doing business. She is underneath him. The CLIENT seems oblivious of the sound of bombs falling outside. He just continues.

LENA

Please, dear God, this one night. Be with us this one night.

CLIENT

What's the matter am I not enough for you?

The explosive force of the bombs outside is powerful enough to knock out half a window. Particles of dust shake out of corner walls, and cups and saucers fall from the edge of the table to the floor.

LENA

You crazy bastard! We're going to die and all you want to do is screw!

CLIENT

Maybe so. But what a way to go.

The plaster from the ceiling shakes and falls away in chunks, thick pieces landing on them. The entire house is filling with SMOKE from the burning houses outside.

LENA pushes him off. And as she pushes him towards the door he gathers up his clothes.

LENA

Not for me it isn't. Get outta here. Go and die someplace else!

She kicks him out and slams the door shut.

The next EXPLOSION rocks the house and sends an uprooted tree crashing against the door, one of its long limbs smashes through the door bringing the CLIENT'S body, impaled, with it. The windows explode into the room. The impact sends LENA against the wall. As the SMOKE clears she sees the horrendous sight of the DEAD MAN.

LENA'S eyes are wide, in terror. She crosses herself.

CUT TO:

147 - INT. PRISON. FRANCESCO'S CELL. NIGHT.

FRANCESCO stares out of his barred window. With every EXPLOSION he sees huge FLASHES coming from a small town nearby.

VOICE

Somebody open these doors.

Other CONS are shouting and screaming to be released.

CUT TO:

148 - EXT. PRISON. NIGHT.

LONG SHOT. The PRISON. We hear a faint WHISTLING getting louder and louder until BANG! It hits the prison. The whole prison shakes.

CUT TO:

149 - INT. PRISON. FRANCESCO'S CELL. NIGHT.

The wall above the bed cracks open, dislodging the bed and knocking FRANCESCO to the center of the cell.

FRANCESCO crawls off the floor and back to his feet. The thick smoke makes breathing difficult. Outside, fire ALARMS ring out in all directions, and everywhere SCREAMS and CRIES can be heard. FRANCESCO walks slowly across the cell, stepping on rubble and stone.

A part of a wall around the cell door has fallen down. Francesco begins to kick away some more of the wall to get enough space to climb out. He then squeezes his way out of the cell.

CUT TO:

150 - INT. PRISON. CORRIDOR. NIGHT.

The corridor is filled with smoke and dust. DEAD BODIES lie under rubble everywhere. Smoke and fire fill the area. FRANCESCO is joined by CHIESA. Together they make their way down the corridor. They can just about see through the smoke.

All around them, CONS run round in panic. As FRANCESCO and CHIESA go past Angelo's cell they look in.

ANGELO'S leg sticks out from under some rubble.

ANGELO

Somebody help me.

FRANCESCO goes in.

FRANCESCO

He's alive, Chiesa!

CUT TO:

151 - INT. PRISON. ANGELO'S CELL. NIGHT.

FRANCESCO and CHIESA try to get a wooden beam off ANGELO. Just then another bomb hits the prison. FRANCESCO and CHIESA fall down then get up again. ANGELO SCREAMS.

ANGELO

Mother of God.

FRANCESCO

**Don't panic. Chiesa, help me with this beam. We haven't much
time.**

FRANCESCO and CHIESA gather their strength for two more lifts,
taking deep, smoke-filled breaths each time. They lift it up and
ANGELO crawls out. The air-raid alarm blows four times.

CHIESA

They've stopped bombing.

FRANCESCO, silently stares out through a cracked window at the
ruin left by the bombs. ANGELO interrupts his stare.

ANGELO

Francesco! Let's get outta here.

152 - INT. PRISON CORRIDOR. NIGHT.

The THREE COMRADES head down another corridor. Running,
FRANCESCO almost trips over a DEAD GUARD. He takes the gun
from the DEAD GUARD'S holster. CHIESA snatches up a shotgun.
The THREE COMRADES make their way down the corridor.

CUT TO:

153 - EXT. PRISON. YARD. NIGHT.

The THREE COMRADES stop by the gates. They gasp for breath.
Then climb over.
CUT TO:

154 - EXT. VILLAGE. NIGHT.

The THREE COMRADES run down a cobbled street. All around
them are BURNING and DAMAGED buildings.

The THREE COMRADES reach a stone barn. The doors are slightly open.

ANGELO

We can rest in here.

They walk in.

CUT TO:

155 - INT. BARN. NIGHT.

Inside the barn are stacks of hay up to the roof and a few HORSES. The THREE COMRADES enter. FRANCESCO crosses to a horse. He mounts.

FRANCESCO

This is where we part company.

ANGELO

What do you mean part company? What about the people who framed you?

FRANCESCO

Revenge is not my first priority. All I want to do is see my Maria. I know she'll come with me.

CHIESA

Okay. You get your sweetheart and then we'll go kill them.

FRANCESCO

No. I thank you both for your loyalty. I must go. Good luck.

ANGELO and CHIESA break loose a horse each and mount. FRANCESCO smiles at them both. Then he rides out of the barn. CHIESA and ANGELO follow him out.

CUT TO:

156 - EXT. OPEN ROAD. MORNING.

It is a cold day. FRANCESCO rides off the road and up a green slope. Suddenly mortar fire terrifies the HORSE. It arrives without a sound, announced only when it explodes. The HORSE rears up throwing FRANCESCO off and onto the ground. The HORSE gallops away over the green slope.

CUT TO:

157 - EXT. CROSSROADS. DAY

The road curves to a rise, then declines. At a crossroads FRANCESCO sees a farmhouse. A signpost points to Cosenza. He crosses to the farmhouse.

CUT TO:

158 - EXT. FARMHOUSE. DAY.

FRANCESCO knocks on the door. No answer. He steps back and looks up.

FRANCESCO'S POV: Frightened faces stare from the upper windows of the half-shuttered farmhouse. From the barn nearby he hears the sound of a pig screeching. He walks towards the barn.

FRANCESCO peers through the open door of the barn. Something moves catching his eye.

The PIG squeals, waving the bloody stumps of its hind legs. By the wall, next to the mutilated pig, a hooked bloodstained machete rests. He enters.

CUT TO:

159 - INT. BARN. DAY.

FRANCESCO enters and abruptly stops. His eyes widen in disbelief.

FRANCESCO is almost face to face with a GERMAN SOLDIER. The GERMAN SOLDIER holds the pig's bloodied leg with one hand and a rifle in the other hand. In one swift movement, he drops the pig's leg and levels his rifle up to FRANCESCO'S head.

CLOSE UP: A HAND reaches for the hooked bloodstained machete and takes it.

BACK VIEW: GERMAN SOLDIER readies himself to fire. FRANCESCO closes his eyes. The HOOKED MACHETE swings into view.

PULL BACK: We see that it is ANGELO swinging the hooked machete at the GERMAN SOLDIER'S neck. The swipe separates the GERMAN SOLDIER'S head from the shoulders. The headless SOLDIER sinks to his knees. Blood gushes out of his neck.

CHIESA and a SOLDIER wearing an ITALIAN UNIFORM enter. The pig is screeching much louder.

FRANCESCO

Somebody put that poor creature out of its misery!

CHIESA picks up the rifle and shoots the pig through the head.

ANGELO smiles at FRANCESCO.

ANGELO

Pleased to see me?

FRANCESCO

(smiles)

What are you doing here?

ANGELO

We're looking for the resistance. We heard they're in this area. We're going to join them.

FRANCESCO looks at the ITALIAN SOLDIER.

FRANCESCO

Who's he?

ITALIAN SOLDIER steps forward and extends a hand. FRANCESCO accepts it.

ITALIAN SOLDIER

Roberto DeLuca. Ex-soldier, looking for a worthwhile cause. IL Duce made a big mistake joining forces with the Germans.

CUT TO:

160 - EXT. COUNTRY ROAD. DAY

Mortars, artillery, rifle and machine gunfire blurs into one demonic howl. Resistance FIGHTERS and BLACK SHIRTS are engaged in battle. They fire at one another from behind rocks and trees across a dirt track road.

The leader of the resistance fighters is BERTI. BERTI is very accurate, shooting several BLACK SHIRTS.

From behind a HAY WAGON, several resistance FIGHTERS fire their weapons at the BLACK SHIRTS. Suddenly a great BLAST shakes the ground. Shrapnel and splintered wood rains down. The HAY WAGON crackles in flames. Several MEN behind it lie in twisted postures. A YOUNG MAN is doubled up, sobbing obscenities as he tries to push his intestines back into his stomach.

Two trucks full of GERMAN INFANTRYMEN screeches to a stop nearby. The infantrymen leap from the vehicles and begin firing at the resistance FIGHTERS. The odds now swing in the black shirts favour. BERTI crouches behind a stump.

BERTI

It's hopeless. Hold your fire.

We surrender.

BERTI stands, holding up a white handkerchief. A dozen of his MEN throw out their weapons and come out with their hands above their heads.

CUT TO:

161 - EXT. COUNTRY ROAD. DAY.

FRANCESCO, ANGELO, CHIESA, and DELUCA walk wearily along the road.

ANGELO

The resistance will fix you up with a horse. If we find them.

They come to a bend in the road. They hear the sound of an ENGINE coming from around the bend. Before they can take cover a truck comes round the bend. BLACK SHIRTS and SS INFANTRYMEN leap out of the truck and surround the four men. They are bundled into the back of the truck.

CUT TO:

162 - INT. TRUCK. DAY.

BERTI and other PRISONERS help the four men in. FRANCESCO sits next to BERTI. He gives him a puzzled look.

BERTI

Resistance. What's left of us.

FRANCESCO looks at ANGELO. ANGELO shrugs.

CUT TO:

163 - EXT. CROSSROADS. DAY.

A HUGE TANK moves forward, pushing aside everything in its path. In the turret, a LEATHER-COATED GERMAN OFFICER shoves the goggles up over his cap and watches SS INFANTRYMEN and BLACK SHIRTS prodding ragged files of freshly captured prisoners past his TANK and into a meadow.

CUT TO:

164 - EXT. MEADOW. DAY.

Thirty or so CONVICTS who escaped the previous night are also there. Some stamping their feet against the biting cold. The resistance FIGHTERS are herded in among them.

FRANCESCO stamps his feet on the hard earth and swings his arms to fight off the penetrating cold. His eyes are watery and mucus beaded under his nose. Nearly fifty PRISONERS now stand, their number swelling steadily by new prisoners.

FRANCESCO glances furtively over his shoulder and sees ANGELO, CHIESA and DELUCA huddled close, staring ahead vacantly. DELUCA'S lips are blue with cold and his chin trembles in the collar of his greatcoat. They had about them the stunned dullness of fighting men suddenly reduced to frightened, beaten men.

Two SS INFANTRYMEN in field grey pass close by FRANCESCO, prodding more prisoners into the meadow with kicks and the butts of their guns. FRANCESCO'S eyes play uneasily over them and the TROOPS leaning from the tanks.

FRANCESCO edges himself closer to the reassuring figure of BERTI. BERTI does not stamp or wave his arms. He stands with resolute dignity

BERTI turns a tough, crinkly face to FRANCESCO and winks. The shivering FRANCESCO manages a faint smile.

Suddenly, a fearsome noise, the sound of metal being shredded, drowns out the distant moan of artillery. FRANCESCO looks up at the hugest tank he has ever seen. The other vehicles hurriedly back away to make way for the LEATHER COATED OFFICER. The TANK stops directly in front of FRANCESCO.

He studies the German's face in mute fascination. GERMAN OFFICER, hands on his hips, rocking on his heels, looked down on the hapless INFANTRYMAN.

LEATHER COATED OFFICER

What is going on?

The INFANTRYMAN gestures helplessly towards the hunched figures in the meadow.

INFANTRYMAN

We don't know what to do with the prisoners.

GERMAN OFFICER seizes the rim of the turret and barks out each word.

LEATHER COATED OFFICER
You imbeciles! Can't you follow a simple order?

GERMAN OFFICER turns towards the meadow and looks out over the shivering FIGURES. His chin assumes a cocksure angle. His holster is swiftly unsnapped.
And you don't know what to do aboutthe prisoners, eh?'

FRANCESCO finds himself staring into a pistol barrel. He stares into the OFFICER'S pitiless gaze and at the pistol pointed at his heart.

FRANCESCO looks desperately at BERTI. BERTI yells and dives at him as the shot rings out.

BERTI
Move, man!

Machine-guns instantly, ring out over the meadow as the TROOPS in the tanks, BLACK SHIRTS, and INFANTRYMEN open fire.

ANGELO, CHIESA, DELUCA, and a handful of MEN at the rear make for nearby sheltering trees. Hoarse screams and cries for mercy fills the meadow as the guns begin to cut down the rest of the men.

FRANCESCO is flung to the ground by BERTI'S huge body. He feels something warm on his face. He tries to twist from under BERTI'S weight to escape the geyser of blood pumping from BERTI'S neck. His dead eyes stare at FRANCESCO, disbelieving.

Guns FIRE from all over. From tank turrets, BLACK SHIRTS and SS INFANTRYMEN standing alongside the meadow, firing as if in a shooting gallery. Some CONVICTS throw up their arms, pleading their helplessness. Still, the guns pour on the fire.

Agonizing screams fill the air and bodies begin to form clumps in the meadow.

Other MEN in the rear flee for the safety of the nearby wood, bullets tearing holes in their backs.

A bullet burrows next to FRANCESCO'S head. He curls up, pretending to be hit. The meadow is a mass of bloody MEN, some writhing, some still.

A YOUNG CONVICT is almost into the trees. A MACHINE-GUNNER raises his sights. The first slug catches him in the thigh. The next exits through his kneecap.

CUT TO:

164A – EXT. FOREST. DAY.
The YOUNG CONVICT stumbles into the woods. ANGELO, CHIESA and DELUCA make it into the trees. They collapse to the ground, panting in deep grotesque gasps.

ANGELO runs close to the ground towards the writhing YOUNG CONVICT. He takes him by the arms, dragging him on his back, as he shrieks hysterically. He pulls him behind a tree, next to CHIESA and DELUCA.
DELUCA rips away the YOUNG CONVICT'S bloodstained trouser leg, exposing the shattered knee. With the ripped material he ties

a tourniquet above the YOUNG CONVICT'S thigh. In the distance, the guns cease firing.

CUT TO:

164B – EXT. MEADOW. DAY.

A pall of smoke drifts Over the meadow. FRANCESCO lies still maintaining a corpse's broken posture. His sham is abetted by BERTI who is dead over him.

The GERMAN OFFICER clambers down from the turret of the TANK, his pistol still in his hand. A half dozen other MEN follow him.

CLOSE UP: FRANCESCO'S FACE. He can hear them LAUGHING, then pistol shots and GROANS. His eyes widen then close as he hears their approaching footsteps.

A BLACK SHIRT stands above him. The BLACK SHIRT pushes BERTI Off FRANCESCO'S back with his foot. He shoots BERTI through the head then aims at FRANCESCO'S head. He pulls the trigger. CLICK! The pistol is empty. He reloads. He points the gun at FRANCESCO.

FRANCESCO'S eyes flick open. He stares at the BLACK SHIRT. BLACK SHIRT is shocked, staring back at FRANCESCO. His gun-hand trembles.
GERMAN OFFICER'S VOICE. FRANCESCO closes his eyes.

GERMAN OFFICER (o.s)

(shouts)

Let's go.

BLACK SHIRT looks at FRANCESCO'S perfectly still body, then turns away and walks off. As he does so he can't help but look back at FRANCESCO.

Gradually, the logjam of iron and men begin to break up and the din of departing engines fading.

DISSOLVE TO:

165 - EXT. MEADOW. NIGHT.

FRANCESCO stands and carefully walks around the CORPSES and onto the road.

CUT TO:

166 - EXT. COSENZA. NIGHT

The street is deserted. FRANCESCO walks at a fast pace.

Two trucks full of GERMAN SOLDIERS comes down the street. FRANCESCO moves into the shadows of a building and stops.

CUT TO:

167 - INT. LENA'S HOUSE. NIGHT.

The bomb-damaged door is roughly repaired with odd pieces of wood nailed into it. LENA sits quietly at a table. There is a slight tap at the window. She gets up and goes to the window. She looks out and sees nothing.

LENA

Who is it?

She goes to the door and opens it. FRANCESCO steps in and closes the door. LENA is in shock.

LENA

Francesco. They told me you
were dead.

He goes to her and hugs her. As his legs give way she holds him
up.

DISSOLVE TO:

168 - INT. LENA'S HOUSE. NIGHT.

FRANCESCO sits at the table. LENA brings him a hot drink.

FRANCESCO

**I gotta thank you for what you tried to do for me in court. You
risked your freedom for me. Why?**

LENA doesn't answer. She smiles warmly and sits opposite him.

LENA

What matters is that you're out of that hell hole.

FRANCESCO

**Yes. And into another. Looks like your place took a hammering
too.**

LENA

**At least that snake, Mori was blown to smithereens. His place
took a direct hit. Everyone knew he got Franco's old bar for
testifying against you.**

FRANCESCO

There is a God, then.

There is a knock at the door. FRANCESCO and LENA exchange a startled look. She goes to the door.

LENA

Who is it?

VOICE

A friend.

LENA

I've got no friends. Go away.

VOICE

Well you got a friend now. Open the door.

LENA

Do I know you?

VOICE

No. But I know you. Or should I say I've heard a lot about you
from my good friend, Francesco.

FRANCESCO smiles. He goes past LENA and opens the door. ANGELO enters. His eyes fall on FRANCESCO.

ANGELO

Francesco. You made it.

FRANCESCO

Am I pleased to see you.
(they hug)
Where's Chiesa?

ANGELO

**I left him, DeLuca, and a few others
up at the caves. We're the new
resistance. We need some food.**

ANGELO looks at LENA.
She's as beautiful as you said.

LENA
(smiles)
**I'll pack some food for you. Those kind
of lies will get all the food you need.**

CUT TO:

169 - INT. MARIA'S ROOM. NIGHT.

MARIA is asleep on her bed. There is a tap on her window. Then another. She stirs. She looks at the window, expectantly. Then she springs off the bed and goes to the window. She opens it. FRANCESCO is there. He climbs in. She almost faints. He catches her. He embraces her. She looks up at him and instinctively kisses him on the mouth. He kisses her back. They break apart.

MARIA
You've come. I thought I was dreaming.

FRANCESCO
Nothing could keep me away from you.

MARIA
I'm ready to go anywhere with you.

FRANCESCO smiles and kisses her again.

CUT TO:

170 - EXT. MOUNTAIN. NIGHT.

The silhouettes of TWO HORSES ride against a star studded sky and a huge silver moon.

CUT TO:

171 - EXT. MOUNTAIN CAVE. NIGHT.

A fire is burning. FRANCESCO and MARIA are naked. They make love with a passion they did not know existed until now.

CUT TO:

172 - INT. DE'ANDRIA MANSION. STUDY. DAY.

PACULA is on the telephone. DON DE'ANDRIA sits at his desk. He is in a dark mood. MAFALDA stands looking desperate.

PACULA

What do you mean you can't tell me? Do you know whom you are talking to?!

PACULA listens then hangs up the phone. He turns to DON DE'ANDRIA.

PACULA

The prison was bombed last night. They don't know how many aredead. Or if anyone got away.

DON DE'ANDRIA slams his fist on the desk.

DON DE'ANDRIA

I knew it! It had to be Acciardi. He has kidnapped my daughter. I want a price put on his head. Fifty thousand Lire for the man who brings me Francesco Acciardi. Dead or alive.

CUT TO:

173 - RAPID MONTAGE.

Posters of the reward, with Francesco's face on them, are posted in various places around Cosenza.

CUT TO:

174 - INT. MOUNTAIN CAVE. NIGHT

FRANCESCO and MARIA sit around a fire.

MARIA

I am so happy, Francesco. You can't begin to imagine how much I missed you. Papa will have people looking for us.

FRANCESCO

Well they'll have their work cut out. We leave tonight for Naples. There we'll board a ship leaving for America.

They kiss and as they do so they hear faint voices coming from afar. FRANCESCO goes out.

CUT TO:

175 - EXT. MOUNTAIN CAVE. NIGHT.

FRANCESCO looks down the mountain. He sees MEN holding lanterns coming up the mountain. He hurries back in.

FRANCESCO (o.s)

Maria get your things we're leaving. Hurry.

CUT TO:

176 - EXT. FOREST. NIGHT.

FRANCESCO and MARIA ride furiously through the trees and bush.

CUT TO:

177 - EXT. FARMHOUSE/FOREST. NIGHT.

FRANCESCO and MARIA ride past the farm house and back into the forest. MARIA pulls up her horse. FRANCESCO stops.

FRANCESCO

What's wrong?

MARIA

I can't go on. I must rest. I don't feel too good.
She looks worn out. He touches her forehead.

FRANCESCO

You have a fever. Come. Get down.

He helps her down.

That farmhouse we passed. That's Tonio's place. I'll go and see
if he'll put us up.

He kisses her forehead.

CUT TO:

178 - INT. TONIO'S BARN. NIGHT.

TONIO is milking a COW. He sits on a stool. FRANCESCO enters. He grabs TONIO'S shoulder. TONIO jumps, squirting the milk all over his boots.

TONIO

Francesco! You scared the shit out of me. I thought it was the
Germans.

FRANCESCO looks at TONIO'S milk-stained boots.

FRANCESCO

(LAUGHS)

Strange colored shit.

TONIO

I thought you were a guest of the authorities. What happened?

FRANCESCO

It's a long story. I need a favour, Tonio. I need a place to stay for a few hours.

TONIO

No problem. Come over to the house.

FRANCESCO

No. I don't want your family to know I'm here.

TONIO

Suit yourself. You hear about Ruggiero? He got called up.

FRANCESCO

What about you?

TONIO

(LAUGHS)

Athlete's foot.

(beat)

Look I've gotta deliver the milk into town. Make yourself at home - with the cows. I'll see you later.

FRANCESCO spies a long black coat hanging on the barn door.

FRANCESCO

One more thing, Tonio. I need that coat.

TONIO

Help yourself.

CUT TO:

179 - EXT. COSENZA. DAIRY. NIGHT.

TONIO steers the horse drawn milk cart to the entrance. Just as he passes the gate his eye are drawn to the reward poster. His POV: FRANCESCO'S PHOTO with the wording: WANTED DEAD OR ALIVE 50,000 LIRE. He turns the horse sharply causing the cart to almost overturn. Milk churns fall to the ground spilling milk everywhere. He rides back.

CUT TO:

180 - INT. TONIO'S BARN. NIGHT.

FRANCESCO helps MARIA down to a bed of hay. She starts shivering.

MARIA

I'm so tired. Just a few hours sleep and I'll be fine.
It's so cold.

FRANCESCO touches her forehead again. She is still shivering.

FRANCESCO

You're boiling. I'm going to get a doctor. Lay down and sleep.

She lays down. FRANCESCO takes off the long black coat and puts it over MARIA. She looks up at him as if it's the last time she'll ever see him.

MARIA

I love you.

He kisses her.

FRANCESCO

I love you.

He exits.

CUT TO:

181 - EXT. TONIO'S FARMHOUSE. NIGHT.

TONIO comes out and heads for the barn. He holds a rifle. He enters the barn.

CUT TO:

182 - INT. BARN. NIGHT.

TONIO'S POV: A FIGURE, covered by a long black coat, asleep in the hay. He lifts up the rifle, takes aim, and FIRES twice.

The FIGURE slightly jerks then is still.

TONIO hurries out.

CUT TO:

183 - EXT. COUNTRY ROAD. NIGHT.

FRANCESCO rides, closely followed by the DOCTOR.

CUT TO:

184 - EXT. POLICE STATION. NIGHT.

GARGIULO pokes his head out of a top window. He is in his pajamas.

GARGIULO

Tonio. Do you know what time it is?! I hope you have a good reason for waking me.

TONIO is wide eyed.

TONIO

I've killed Francesco Acciardi!

CUT TO:

185 - INT. BARN. NIGHT.

FRANCESCO hurries over to MARIA followed by the DOCTOR. The sight of the BLOOD pouring from the bullet wounds in her back stops him in his tracks. The DOCTOR pushes past him and commences to examine MARIA. After a few moments the DOCTOR turns back to FRANCESCO.

The DOCTOR slowly shakes his head, his eyes never wavering from FRANCESCO.

FRANCESCO falls to his knees. His head goes up and he SCREAMS.

CUT TO:

186 - EXT. BARN. NIGHT.

The DOCTOR rushes out and mounts his horse. FRANCESCO'S scream can still be heard LOUDER still, sounding more INHUMAN with each scream, causing the HORSE to rear up. The DOCTOR brings the horse under control then gallops away.

DISSOLVE TO:

187 - INT. BARN. NIGHT.

FRANCESCO sits with MARIA'S dead body in his arms. Her head is against his chest looking as if she is in a deep sleep. He talks to her. He is distraught.

FRANCESCO

In my dream I hear my brother's muffled shouting. Then when I think I've lost him I run past him somehow; then I see him, almost straight ahead.

(beat)

It always pulls me back, back to my brother Mino and back to that cave; I hear Mino crying out and I can still see him reaching towards me and he's about to slip away from me again and I can't do anything.

(beat)

I had the same dream for years, until I found you.

Tears start rolling down his cheeks, as he continues.

FRANCESCO

When you get to heaven tell Mino there hasn't been a day that I haven't thought of him. And papa,

(beat)

tell papa I forgive him.

(beat)

In prison I was afraid to die. Afraid I'd never see you again. Now I'm afraid to live.

He kisses the top of her head.

CUT TO:

188 - INT. LENA'S HOME. NIGHT.

ANGELO and LENA are in bed. They are asleep. Several knocks on the door awakes them. LENA goes to the door.

LENA

Who's there?

FRANCESCO (o.s)

It's me.

LENA quickly opens the door. FRANCESCO almost falls in, distraught.

LENA

Francesco. What's happened?

ANGELO gets out of bed and starts dressing. FRANCESCO'S voice is trembling.

FRANCESCO

They've taken Maria away from me?

ANGELO

That's not a problem. We'll get her back.

FRANCESCO

You don't understand. She's gone. They killed her!

LENA

Who killed her?

FRANCESCO'S head raises. His look becomes strong. His eyes stare, coldly.

FRANCESCO

All of them.

(beat)

Pacula, Summo, Mazzari, Morandi, the judge, Gargiulo, and De'Andria!

(beat)

When the Devil took Mori he left seven others behind. One by one I'll send them to hell! So help me God!

SILENCE.

FADE TO:

189 - EXT. BARN. NIGHT.

TONIO is next to a POLICEMAN. GARGIULO comes out of the barn. He is followed out by DON DE'ANDRIA who carries the limp body of MARIA. He places her body in the waiting carriage and walks back to TONIO and GARGIULO.

TONIO

What about my reward? 50,000 Lire.

DON DE'ANDRIA stops almost face to face with TONIO. He stares coldly into TONIO'S eyes as his hand pulls out a revolver and fires it simultaneously. Each shot knocks TONIO back until he hits the ground. There are SCREAMS heard from within the farmhouse. Then an OLD WOMAN runs out of the house. The POLICEMAN holds her back.

DON DE'ANDRIA climbs into the carriage. Then it moves off.

CUT TO:

190 - EXT. STREET. NIGHT.

ANGELO and CHIESA see MAZZARI'S car outside the restaurant. They stand outside a bar not far from the car.

ANGELO looks at his watch. Suddenly CHIESA hits ANGELO'S shoulder. They see MAZZARI emerging from the restaurant, caught in the glow of the door lights.

MAZZARI walks to his car. ANGELO slowly walks towards the car and leans against it.
ANGELO waits for MAZZARI to go past, then smiles politely to let him get into his car. When MAZZARI is inside, ANGELO pulls out his gun.

MAZZARI is about to put his key into the ignition, his car window down, raises his eyes.

ANGELO

Francesco Acciardi, says hello.

At the moment ANGELO fires, they look into each other's eyes.

MAZZARI is frozen as the bullet smashes into his eye.

ANGELO flings the door open and fires again.

CUT TO:

191 - EXT. SUMMA HOME. NIGHT.

Two POLICEMEN guard the house.

FIRST POLICEMAN

Got a cigarette?

SECOND POLICEMAN takes out a packet and hands him a cigarette. As he lights it.

LENA (o.s)

Got one for me?

They turn their attention on her. In the background FRANCESCO slips quietly around the back.

CUT TO:

192 - INT. SUMMA HOME. NIGHT.

Summo is in bed, asleep. FRANCESCO is in the room. A walks over to the bed and stands over him. He shakes SUMMA. SUMMA stirs and opens his eyes. In the darkness he can barely see.

SUMMA

Who's there?

FRANCESCO

It's the Devil. That is the way you described me in court, isn't it?

FRANCESCO wraps a cord around SUMMA'S neck and strangles him.

Now you'll never tell another lie!

CUT TO:

193 - EXT. SUMMA HOME. NIGHT.

FIRST POLICEMAN touches LENA'S mouth.

FIRST POLICEMAN

You know how to use that?

SECOND POLICEMAN

Of course she does. That's what she's here for.

CHIESA and ANGELO come from behind. CHIESA wraps a cord around the FIRST POLICEMEN'S neck and strangles him. At the same time ANGELO cuts the other COP'S throat. The two COPS fall to the ground. ANGELO looks down at the dead COPS.

ANGELO

Don't you know you shouldn't mess with another man's woman!

LENA

You really mean that?

ANGELO

Of course. God help anyone who touches you again.

ANGELO smiles at her. She returns the smile.

FRANCESCO comes out. And they all move off down the road.

CUT TO:

194 - INT. MORANDI HOME. NIGHT.

CHIESA

How many other poor bastards have you helped to frame for Don De'Andria?

MORANDI'S face flushes red.

MORANDI

You think you can scare me. I'll have you thrown back into jail.

CHIESA bangs on the door. FRANCESCO enters. MORANDI'S eyes widen.

MORANDI

You! You're supposed to be dead?

FRANCESCO

No, that's you. You're the dead man.

MORANDI stands and tries to run past him.

Then suddenly FRANCESCO pulls MORANDI to him. And as they break apart MORANDI flops to his knees. Half his shirt has been sliced away. A gush of blood pours from his stomach.

FRANCESCO'S holds the knife, the blood crimson on its broad blade up to the hilt.

CUT TO

195 - EXT. VILLAGE. NIGHT.

The night of Saint Anthony's fancy-dress fiesta is in progress. The whole town is there dressed up. A live band is playing loud happy music. PEOPLE are eating, drinking and dancing.

The THREE COMRADES, all three wearing customary masks, mingle in with the happy CROWD. They stop and lean against a wall looking at the DANCERS.

Nearby, outside a bar, GARGIULO sits at a table with some of his UNIFORMED POLICEMEN.

The THREE MASKED COMRADES focus on GARGIULO.

GARGIULO stands and goes to the back of the bar.

CUT TO:

196 - EXT. BACK OF THE BAR. NIGHT.

It is dark. GARGIULO stops by a wall and unzips his trousers. He starts to urinate against the wall. FRANCESCO joins him. GARGIULO without looking at FRANCESCO.

GARGIULO

Good evening. And a fine one it is.

FRANCESCO

Yes it is. But not for you!

GARGIULO recognises FRANCESCO'S voice, turns quickly to him.

GARGIULO

But you're dead!

FRANCESCO

No, that's you. Time to die!

FRANCESCO holds a gun. He opens fire. GARGIULO still holding his penis, falls to the ground.

FRANCESCO

You're the second piece of shit tonight to get it wrong.

CUT TO:

<u>197 - EXT. BAR. NIGHT.</u>

The music stops and the CROWDS begin to panic. People SCREAM and run everywhere. Before the POLICEMEN at the table can react, ANGELO and CHIESA are upon them.

CHIESA and ANGELO FIRE their guns. The POLICEMEN fall in a hail of bullets.

FRANCESCO joins CHIESA and ANGELO. They escape.
FADE TO:

198 - EXT. CHURCH. DAY.

The rain falls steadily. EIGHT MEN carry Maria's coffin out and slide it into the waiting hearse. The hearse is covered in flowers.

The hearse moves slowly away followed by DON DE'ANDRIA, MAFALDA, who sobs constantly, ANNA, PACULA, JUDGE PIRLO, FURIO, MANNO, and TWENTY BLACK SHIRTS. Behind them follow hundreds of village folk, some with umbrellas and some sharing umbrellas.

DON DE'ANDRIA tries to comfort his wife. He puts an arm around her shoulder. She pushes it violently away.

MAFALDA

Don't touch me! It is all your fault Maria is dead.

She sobs and walks on. DON DE'ANDRIA looks at her vacantly.

The RAIN dances a faster beat as the CORTEGE makes its way down the road.

CUT TO:

199 - EXT. ROOFTOP. DAY.

FRANCESCO stands, soaking wet, looking down on the CORTEGE.

FADE OUT:

200 - INT. DE'ANDRIA'S MANSION. STUDY. NIGHT.

DON DE'ANDRIA sits at his desk. He stares at the half glass of brandy. He is SILENT. PACULA is on the phone. JUDGE PIRLO stands nervously looking out of the window. All three are still in their black attire.

PACULA

What the hell is going on? You assured me he was dead!

(listens)

I don't care where he is, get Puntina over here!

He hangs up. DON DE'ANDRIA picks up the glass and downs the brandy. He opens his desk drawer and pulls out a revolver. He checks the chambers and puts it back in the drawer and closes it. He pours another brandy.

JUDGE PIRLO

He's killed them all. We need protection. He won't stop until he gets us too.

PACULA

Sit down and shut up. I have twenty men watching the house. He won't get past them.

CUT TO:

<u>201 - EXT. DE'ANDRIA'S MANSION. GATES. NIGHT.</u>
A CAR drives in. BLACK SHIRTS stand in the driveway. The car stops.

A BLACK SHIRT shines a torch in the driver's face. It is PUNTINA. They wave him on.

CUT TO:

<u>202 - EXT. DE'ANDRIA'S MANSION. NIGHT.</u>
FRANCESCO walks quietly over the patio, onto the grass and towards the DE'ANDRIA MANSION. CHIESA, DELUCA and

165

ANGELO follow close behind. Suddenly the FLOODLIGHTS come on.

VOICE

You are surrounded put down yourweapons and surrender.

FRANCESCO

Let's go!

They FIRE their guns at the FLOODLIGHTS smashing one then another. There follows a ferocious battle.

CUT TO:

203 - INT. DE'ANDRIA'S MANSION. STUDY. NIGHT.

On hearing the gunshots, PUNTINA and PACULA move to the window. JUDGE PIRLO hides with his back to the wall, away from the windows. DON DE'ANDRIA does not react he continues to drink.

JUDGE PIRLO

I can't stand anymore of this. I'm going out to Acciardi. I'll tell him everything.

PACULA turns away from the window and faces the JUDGE.

PACULA

And you think he'll let you live?

JUDGE PIRLO

He will when he hears what I have to say.
It wasn't my idea to frame him but yours and Luciano.

JUDGE PIRLO makes for the door. PUNTINA moves across from the window to the door. He grabs JUDGE PIRLO and swings him back in. He produces a pistol and raises it to the JUDGE'S head. PUNTINA stands with his back to the open door.

Just as PUNTINA points the gun at the JUDGE he feels another gun pressing at the back of his head. He freezes.

FRANCESCO'S VOICE
I should just let you plug him. But I want that satisfaction.

DON DE'ANDRIA opens his desk draw and pulls out the pistol.

FRANCESCO
Now I'll ask just once, who killed Maria?

DON DE'ANDRIA
I did.

DON DE'ANDRIA puts the pistol into his mouth and FIRES. The back of his skull EXPLODES. He falls back on his chair his eyes wide staring at the ceiling. JUDGE PIRLO tries to save his skin.

JUDGE PIRLO
Acciardi! Kill that bastard like he killed your father.

PACULA stares at the lifeless DON DE'ANDRIA. Then turns back to JUDGE PIRLO.

PACULA
Be quiet.

JUDGE PIRLO
Yes. It's true, Acciardi. Your father never hung himself.

FRANCESCO
Is that true, Puntina?

PUNTINA still stands pointing the gun at JUDGE PIRLO. And with FRANCESCO'S gun at the back of his head, he nods.

PUNTINA
I was just following orders.

PACULA
Don't listen to him.

JUDGE PIRLO
Yes. Your father never hung himself. Puntina did it. He was ordered by Ricardo Pacula.
(beat)
Pacula knew your father would get off. No jury in the land would have convicted him for what he did.

FRANCESCO
But why?

PUNTINA
Your father had always been a pain in Pacula's ass. Honest cops never did get on with Pacula. Especially cops who hated Fascists.

FRANCESCO is confused.

FRANCESCO
(to himself)
So my father didn't leave us.

PACULA

You bastard!

PACULA rushes forward pushing PUNTINA'S gun hand. The gun FIRES hitting JUDGE PIRLO between the eyes.

PUNTINA swings the gun back and shoots PACULA. PACULA drops like a sack of potatoes. At the same time PUNTINA swings round and knocks the gun out of FRANCESCO'S hand.

FRANCESCO runs forward pushing PUNTINA back towards the window. They both crash through it.

CUT TO:

204 - EXT. DE'ANDRIA'S MANSION. NIGHT.
FRANCESCO and PUNTINA crash out of the window and into the garden.

As FRANCESCO tries to get up all the lights come on. The garden is swarming with POLICE and BLACK SHIRTS. He sees CHIESA, and ANGELO handcuffed. DELUCA dead on the ground. From behind him PUNTINA crashes a club across his head.

CUT TO:

205 - INT. OUTSIDE PERICARDI'S OFFICE. EVENING.
The door opens and TWO GUARDS carry FRANCESCO out by his arms and legs. He is half-unconscious. His head BLEEDS from a cut above his ear, trailing BLOOD across the floor.

PUNTINA and DELGADO follow them out. PERICARDI looks down the corridor after them. Then looks at the trail of BLOOD, He shakes his head and goes back into his office, closing the door behind him.

CUT TO:

206 - INT. PRISON. CELL. EVENING.

Door opens. They dump FRANCESCO into the cell. DELGADO and PUNTINA follow the TWO GUARDS into the cell.

DELGADO and PUNTINA beat FRANCESCO systematically with their clubs and kick him with their boots. They fracture and tear part of his scalp and gouge out his right eye almost out of its socket. By the time they finish the cell is full of BLOOD.

CUT TO:

207 - INT. OUTSIDE FRANCESCO'S CELL. EVENING.

PUNTINA watches while DELGADO locks the cell door. PUNTINA nudges him and gestures down the corridor.

ZANETTI walks down the corridor towards them. He reaches them.

ZANETTI

What's going on? Who's in there? I've had no papers

DELGADO

Don't need any. Orders straight from the governor's office.

ZANETTI looks at the patches of BLOOD by the foot of the door. He opens the PEEPHOLE and looks in.

ZANETTI'S POV: Through the shaft of light which shines on FRANCESCO'S face he sees him lying in a deep coma, his skull laid bare, one eye goggling out. He gapes too horrified to move for the moment. He takes an involuntary step backwards as, DELGADO LAUGHS. PUNTINA copies him.

CUT TO:

208 - INT. OUTSIDE PERICARDI'S OFFICE. EVENING.

PADRE PINO walks briskly down the corridor. He reaches the door and stops. Just as he is about to burst in, the door opens and A CON steps out. He carries a mop and bucket. From within WE HEAR ZANETTI and PERICARDI'S VOICES, They are arguing furiously with each other. PADRE PINO stops the door swinging shut and listens for a moment.

PERICARDI (o.s)

Your father was a fine guard because he knew how to deal with these animals.

ZANETTI(o.s)

Don't give me anymore bullshit about my father!

CUT TO:

209 - INT. PERICARDI'S OFFICE. EVENING.

PERICARDI sits behind his desk. ZANETTI stands facing him. DELGADO and PUNTINA are behind him.

ZANETTI

Just tell me how to deal with animals like Puntina and Delgado!

PUNTINA moves for ZANETTI but stops as the door swings open. PADRE PINO enters. SILENCE.

PERICARDI, ZANETTI, DELGADO, and PUNTINA watch PADRE PINO as he studies the STAINED carpet. He crosses to the desk. PERICARDI stands. PERICARDI and PADRE PINO stand on either side of the desk.

PADRE PINO

I've got just one thing to say to you; if you don't take Acciardi immediately to the infirmary I'll personally file criminal charges against you!

PERICARDI sits down again. He shares a look with PUNTINA, then he turns back to the PRIEST. He gulps.

PADRE PINO brings up his clenched fist. A FINGER flicks out, pointing at PERICARDI.

PADRE PINO

Now you feel the fear of God!

DISSOLVE TO:

210 - INT. PRISON. CORRIDOR. NIGHT.

PUNTINA walks down the dimly lit corridor. He holds a ROPE, one end of which is knotted to form a noose.

CUT TO:

211 - INT. PRISON. CELL BLOCK. NIGHT.

A PAIR OF UNIFORMED LEGS walk along the tier. The unlocking of a cell DOOR. Then another. Then another.

RUSSO comes out of his cell. ANGELO joins him. Then by SEVERAL other CONS. Soon there are HUNDREDS of CONS. They creep along the tier.

CUT TO:

212 - INT. PRISON. CELL BLOCK. NIGHT.

ZANETTI walks along the corridor. He HEARS, WHACKS, THUDS, and GRUNTS from the upper tier. He hurries up the stairs and peers through the PEEPHOLE down the long, dingy corridor. Through the PEEPHOLE: VINCI walking down the corridor.

From out of the shadows at the end of the tier CHIESA and another CON, with lead pipes in their hands, are creeping up on VINCI. They leap and the lead pipes flash up.

VINCI hears a sound behind him, straightens up a little, half turns. The lead pipes slash down. One catches him full in the face. The other caves in the side of his skull.

He goes rigid, sways, BLOOD spurts. The PIPES hit him again. He is dead before he hits the floor.
CUT TO:

213 - EXT. PRISON. THE YARD. NIGHT.

RUSSO follows, watching DELGADO'S every move. He starts walking faster to catch up with his prey.

A bolt of lightning lights the sky. A CLAP OF THUNDER shakes the chapel windows.

DELGADO senses he's being followed. He picks up his pace. So does RUSSO.

DELGADO ducks behind some steps. In a few seconds, RUSSO arrives. DELGADO steps out in front of him, blocking his path.

They stare at one another in hostility. Then CHIESA appears. He prods DELGADO'S back. DELGADO turns.

A bolt of lightning lights up CHIESA'S face briefly, as:

> DELGADO
>
> **You!**

Fear strikes DELGADO'S face, A CLAP OF THUNDER reverberates in the distance. It begins to rain.

RUSSO smiles malevolently. DELGADO looks down and sees a long blade in CHIESA'S hand.

CLOSE UP: CHIESA'S HAND, it holds the long blade.

HANDS grapple for the blade. DELGADO and CHIESA struggle. SOFT THUDS piercing material and flesh. From behind, RUSSO slits DELGADO'S throat with a blade.

CUT TO:

214 - INT. PERICARDI'S OFFICE. NIGHT.

PERICARDI sits behind his desk sifting through some papers. He is startled by the SOUND of many FOOTSTEPS approaching his office. He looks at the door. An enormous THUD and the door caves in. It comes off its hinges. In the doorway are a CROWD of CONS. One CON holds a ROPE.

PERICARDI in shock.

CUT TO:

215 - INT. PRISON. CELL BLOCK. NIGHT.

ZANETTI staggers back. He slips away down the stairs, shaking, stumbling. The urge to vomit fights in his guts with a horrifying thrill.

CUT TO:

216 - EXT. PRISON. THE YARD. NIGHT.

ZANETTI comes down the stairs two and three at a time. He stumbles near the bottom. He rolls on the ground.

As he gets up he first sees the legs and bottom of DELGADO'S trousers then his face.

DELGADO lies on the floor, his face distorted, his throat is cut, and his club showing half out of his mouth. ZANETTI vomits
CUT TO:

217 – INT. PRISON. OUTSIDE FRANCESCO'S CELL. NIGHT.

PUNTINA stops outside the cell door. He places the rope under his arm. He produces a bunch of keys and unlocks the door.

CUT TO:

218 - INT. FRANCESCO'S CELL. NIGHT.

SIMULATED DARKNESS: PUNTINA enters. The dim light falls on FRANCESCO'S bed. He is unconscious.

PUNTINA smiles and crosses to the bed. He lifts up the rope and throws it over a beam. Suddenly PUNTINA freezes. He senses he is not alone. Suddenly several hands grab him. There is an almighty struggle. Then SILENCE.

CUT TO:

219 - EXT. FRANCESCO'S CELL. NIGHT.

The door opens and out comes ANGELO and several CONS. Two CONS carry FRANCESCO out on a stretcher. FRANCESCO'S good eye opens. His POV. The open door of the cell. PUNTINA hanging by his neck. Hands tied behind his back. His legs kick for a moment then they are still.

CUT TO:

220 - EXT. PRISON. INFIRMARY. NIGHT.

The rain pours down heavily as the TWO CONS carry FRANCESCO on a stretcher to the INFIRMARY.

FADE TO:

221 - INT. PRISON. INFIRMARY. DAY.

FRANCESCO is lying on a bed, his head is heavily bandaged and a patch is over his right eye. He stirs and opens his eye to find PADRE PINO standing by his bed smiling down at him.

PADRE PINO

Welcome back. We thought we'd lost you.

He moves his head to the other side of the bed and LENA stands there. She smiles at him. FRANCESCO painfully forces himself up. He smiles at them both.

PADRE PINO

You'll soon be out of here, Francesco. Pericardi signed a full confession. He was on De'Andria's payroll. Apparently anybody who got in De'Andria and Pacula's way ended up in here.

LENA

You don't have to be afraid anymore, Francesco. You're a free man.

FRANCESCO

What is life without Maria?

PADRE

Life goes on my son. When one chapter ends we start another.
(beat)
Didn't you once say to me something about America?

FADE TO:

222 - EXT. CEMETARY. DAY.

FRANCESCO, with a packed suitcase down by his side, stands by Maria's marble tomb. The bandages are off. The patch is off. And his right eye is healed but badly disfigured. He places a bouquet of flowers down on the marble. LENA also places flowers down. While PADRE PINO watches them.

LONG SHOT. They hug and kiss one another on the cheek. He walks away holding the suitcase.

FADE OUT

THE END